TONY WILLIAMS grew up in M
a decade in Sheffield and now lives in Alnwick in Northumberland. He teaches creative writing at Northumbria University, but previously worked as an environmental charity worker, dogsbody in a French restaurant, and custodian of a disused lead mine. He was also a failed child wrestler. He writes poetry and prose fiction. His first collection of poetry, *The Corner of Arundel Lane and Charles Street,* was published by Salt in 2009 and shortlisted for the Aldeburgh First Collection Prize and the Portico Prize for Literature.

Also by Tony Williams

The Corner of Arundel Lane and Charles Street

To Keith

Best wishes at Colpitts

April '13

TONY WILLIAMS

Tony Williams

ALL THE BANANAS I'VE NEVER EATEN

TALES OF LOVE AND LONELINESS

SALT

CROMER

PUBLISHED BY SALT PUBLISHING
12 Norwich Road, Cromer, Norfolk NR27 0AX

© Tony Williams, 2012

The right of Tony Williams to be identified as the author
of this work has been asserted by him in accordance with
Section 77 of the Copyright, Designs and Patents Act 1988.

Salt Publishing 2012

Printed in the UK by TJ International Ltd, Padstow, Cornwall

Typeset in Paperback 9/13

ISBN 978 1 84471 321 9 paperback

1 3 5 7 9 8 6 4 2

CONTENTS

CLICKS

Collard gave us a load of trundlewheels and took us out on the field to measure distances. I went over the fence at the back and kept trundling.

There's no discreet way to steal a trundlewheel. You just push it along in front of you. If anybody asked, you'd say it was a project. But they wouldn't ask.

I reached the Spar at the corner and turned into the estate. Counting. Every time the wheel goes round it clicks, and that's a metre. Wrapped round the edge of the wheel. Collard showed us. I counted 326 metres to the Spar from the school fence. Fifteen from there to the post box. Post box to Wood's house: 37 metres. But you don't say metres. You say *clicks*.

That's what they say in *Full Metal Jacket*. I watched it with Wood's cousin at Christmas. 'Contact with Charlie. Forty clicks.' And so on.

Lampposts every twenty-five clicks. Eight clicks up the garden path and eight clicks down again when no one answered the door. Six hundred and twenty-seven clicks between my house and the hospital. Four hundred and eight clicks from the hospital to the police station. Nobody stopped me. Ninety-two clicks is how far I ran from Biggsy when my sister slapped him. I reckon the trail of blood was forty-five clicks but the rain had washed it away so I had to — *estimate*.

Nineteen clicks past the last house the tarmac ends. Seventy clicks of dusty track. It was hard to keep the wheel steady through the tussocks, but something like thirty-nine clicks to the bottom of the field.

I climbed up on the fence and wanged the trundlewheel into the river. No more clicks then, just the trickly sound of the water. And that's just right—the river moves but it stays where it is, the trundlewheel goes downriver surrounded by the same patch of water.

MOVEMENTS

I got into the whole traveller thing because of Molly. She was a full-on crusty: blonde dreads, dog on a string, and so on. I met her outside the Pig O'Lead and didn't sleep in a house for three years. I joined the camp on Stanton Moor, protesting about the mining, just to please her at first, but I got really into it. It's a world-view; a way of being.

Vegan, scraggy beard, drinking cider, cheap drugs, henna and drumming. I loved it. Her, I suppose. Then one day when the others were having a go at the solstice-and-candles stuff I fixed a circular saw to an old tractor and cut down a lamppost in the retail park. You know, as a statement.

There was this girl watching from the doorway of McDonald's. Dark hair, pale skin, sad eyes. A tiny bit flaccid. Then when I got released on police bail she was there outside the copshop, sitting on a bench, waiting.

'I'm Emma,' she said. 'I've got some things you'll like.'

She took me back to her dad's flat. There were these gadgets — basically scissors mounted on to hoovers — and you could make them go with remotes. We spent the afternoon rigging one up with half a pair of pinking shears and stabbing holes in his sofa, and then we lay on it and did something else so that by the time he got back from work I knew quite a lot about his daughter. He was alright about it though. She'd told him about the lamppost. Next thing I know, our song is Mötley Crüe's 'You're All I Need' and we're auditioning for the third series of *Robot Wars*.

LENGTHS

She must have been desperate to call the home phone. He'll have told her not to. 'Is Ian there?' she says, not even trying to hide the wobble in her voice. 'I . . . I've tried him at the office and they told me he wasn't working today. The thing is I really really need to speak to him.'

Pregnant.

I stare out at the empty drive. 'Have you tried his mobile?'

'Yes but he isn't answering.'

He wouldn't. He goes swimming on a Tuesday morning. 'Well, keep trying,' I say, 'he's bound to pick up some time.'

After I've rung off I boil the kettle. I bang the cupboard doors. I turn off the oven. And when I've made my tea I sit down and sip it, and smile. It amuses me to think of his phone going off and going off, shrill and muffled in that metal locker, while he swims lengths fifty yards away, earplugs in, unaware of the bomb that is about to drop.

C'EST MAGNIFIQUE, MAIS CE N'EST PAS LA GUERRE

I've had it up to here with Josie and her bloody chickens. I love her, but — those chickens. It's not a pet, it's a lifestyle choice. It's a blinking obsession. It's her leaping out of bed at half past six and no slap-and-tickle for me. Not even a cuppa.

This morning I watched her from the window before I jumped in the shower. Shovelling muck, chucking seed down for them. Picking them up, cosseting the little buggers. And that cockerel, Robespierre, strutting around like he owns the place. If I ever get near him I'll throttle him.

When I went downstairs, she bent down and kissed me. She's a big girl, Josie. I love her. But then — going on about these eggs she's put in the incubator — hoping for a new cockerel to replace 'Robbie' — and out the door. No breakfast for me, kettle not even hot, nothing.

She's made up names for all the chicks already, and they haven't hatched yet. They might not even be fertilised. But there, on the notepad I bought her to write her shopping lists: *Louis, Jean-Claude, Gerard*. And, in capitals, *NAPOLEON*, underlined with a silly flourish.

I put the kettle on and bunged a couple of slices of bread in the toaster. Then I went towards the incubator and selected the egg I thought looked most like it contained an emperor.

When the water had boiled I poured it into a shallow pan and added a dash of vinegar, then cracked the egg. It swirled and steamed, the transparent gloop becoming solid white, while I whistled a happy tune and looked to see where she keeps the HP sauce.

WE'RE KAPPA

Becs met Stevie at the newsagents as usual. He had a black eye from the fight with his brother. She kissed it and he said, 'Stink of fags. Give us one,' and she did.

They walked over the bridge into the gravel expanse of the free car park. It was half-empty on a weekday. They kicked stones along between the rows of cars, and Stevie looked in the windows to see if there was anything on the seats. It was quiet out here, away from the roundabout in the town centre. There was the rustle of their tracksuits as they moved. The trees were big and green and lit up and swaying in the spring sun and wind. They sat on the steps of the taxi office and snogged, then smoked another Lambert. Stevie hogged it, and Becs had to beg two's-up even though it was her fag.

They walked down to the river. Becs wanted to ask about his brother and what had happened in Afghanistan, but she didn't dare. Also she wanted to tell Stevie that her mother was getting a dog. Halfway along the river to the next estate they stopped in a clearing. On one side the river gurgled past in a thin brown rush, and on the other was a line of trees, and then a field and then the dual carriageway. Becs sat down and lit another fag, and Stevie stood on the muddy bank throwing sticks into the water.

'Same trackies on again,' he said suddenly, and grinned,

showing his brace. She thought, No shit, Sherlock, but she smiled and put her hands up to her head to smooth back her hair.

'Here,' he said, walked round behind her and sat down with his back to hers. They could feel each others' spines poking against each other. He drew up his knees like hers were, and turned his head to look over her shoulder. 'We're Kappa, you and me. The bloke and and his bird in the Kappa picture.' He held up his arm for her to see the logo repeated all the way down to his mucky cuffs. 'It's like we're a couple, or whatever,' he said. 'It's like it's love.'

She didn't say anything, but leaned her head back against him and took one last long drag on the Lambert before flicking it into the water. They sat in the dappled sunlight. She wondered if he'd brought any condoms. She didn't have any mints to take the taste away. He was thinking about Michael, and last night, and the drinking. He wondered if he'd have the bollocks to show her the other bruises.

ANYA'S COMPLAINT

Anya's beauty was in her hair. She had it tied it up most of the time, sitting in The Plum Pie drinking a gin and bitter lemon, reading her copy of *English Folk Tales* with a faraway look. But everyone knew that when she let it down, for instance for the river-swimming at the summer festival, or at her father's funeral, it reached down past her knees, almost to her feet. In that brown bough of frame her pale face, freckled and elfin, could not help but upset the young men of the village. She was a living rebuke, a medieval picture of innocence. In the water, it spread out in a vast circle so that they couldn't approach her. It was like the stinging fronds of an anemone.

Geoff arrived and they fell in love. He had a job delivering veg boxes for the organic grocer's. At first he smoked roll-ups, but he soon gave that up after he got together with Anya. His hair was the same colour as hers, but wilder. It lay in tufts over his shoulders. He had a bushy beard, and such a quiet voice that it was almost impossible to talk to him at all. But it was the right volume for whispering in Anya's tiny white ears.

She took to wearing her hair down more often, and Geoff grew his hair too, and they walked in the fields outside the village, hand in hand. Anya's hair fell down around her like a priestess's robes.

One afternoon they went to a secluded spot amongst the

beech trees. If anyone had been watching from the hedge-row he would have seen them taking off their clothes and walking, naked, on the crisp remains of last year's leaves. He would have heard Anya say that her breasts were cold. She used that word—*breasts*—and the watcher would have reflected that that's how it was when your girlfriend was ethereal. Perhaps he would have thought that they would put their clothes back on, but instead Geoff reached out his arms and drew her towards him.

He sat cross-legged in the clearing and sat Anya down facing him, then drew her closer so that their faces and bodies became invisible inside a tent of hair. Anya's reached down past her buttocks and lay in pools on the grass and sticks, and she wrapped it round Geoff and over his shoulders, which were fairly well concealed already. (It had turned out, to nobody's surprise, that he had the most tremendously hairy back.) They sat like for a long time. For a while Geoff talked about the seasons on a theme suggested to him by Anya's complaint: natural materials he might use to warm her body or which were suggested by it; locations for a future paradise; and activities therein. Then Anya told him the most secret fears of her childhood, and described in detail the moments when, in her intimacy with Geoff, one by one, each of these fears had been finally laid to rest. Then they sang together for a while, in low voices which were comfortable in their slight tunelessness.

The watchers outside the hair-tent could hear only a low murmur, and none of what was said between Anya and Geoff. They felt ashamed, that they had gone there to see what was not meant to be seen.

In the beer garden later that summer, Briggsy set fire to them for a laugh. It wasn't funny. Geoff managed to slosh his cider over his face and that saved him from the worst of it — it had to be shaved off later, but he wasn't burned. But all of Anya's fabled hair was gone in a second. She had to go off to the county hospital. That wasn't the worst of it — the worst of it was seeing her suddenly bald head, a charred almond, the fear and humiliation and madness in those eyes. It was sickening to see her hauled through the centuries like that. They had to take off her blouse — that was burning too. And Geoff went and tried to hold her, but she was burned so they wouldn't let him, and all he could do was to stand round with the others, crying and cooing. That white skin, marked with red burns.

Everyone condemned what Briggsy had done, and it was right that he went to prison. But we were a bit grateful too. We see Anya in The Plum Pie and ask how she is. She wears a scarf with her velvet jacket, but she doesn't try to hide the scars. Sometimes Geoff's in there on his own, and he'll have a drink and a game of pool. He's alright, a Thin Lizzy fan. We all saw what happened, we see what's underneath now that the hair has gone. We pummel them with friendly gestures. And now they have to share the love.

SUKI'S LETTER

He had developed a fetish for the *fufu* they served at the African café behind the job centre. He'd always been mad for starches, but chippies were such confrontational places. The *fufu* was made of cassava, which he imagined as being a bit like yams. He sat in the corner, stuffing his face, listening to 'Come on you slags' by Aphex Twin, and reading Suki's letter.

She had drawn her own face in black ink, smiling out at him. A few curvy lines showed she had begun to draw her body too, but thought better of it. That was a shame — it would have made a good drawing, and he could imagine it anyway. In his mind the biro scribbled in a little dark triangle. He looked up suddenly and scanned the room. No one was watching: the woman behind the counter was talking on the phone, and a few customers sat at the other tables, but they were ignoring him.

Under the drawing Suki had written some stuff—friendly and self-consciously kooky. It embarrassed and charmed him and made him want to cry, a bit. She seemed to be having a nice time.

On the other side of the letter she had written him some multiple-choice questions. They concerned where he'd been going, what he'd been eating, whether he was still doing the things they used to do. Then:

How are you feeling?
1 Absolutely A-OK thank you Mrs!
2 Er, bit gippy today — too much curry sauce
3 Still totally down and having murderous thoughts, actually

After that was some stuff about if he needed a hug et cetera. But he wasn't reading that. He was staring at the page, and he'd stopped eating the *fufu*. It had occurred to him to answer the question, and he was thinking about what he should answer.

He imagined Suki getting the letter back. She would probably be in company. He hoped she would put the letter away and read it alone, later, but suspected she wouldn't. He imagined her reading his answer, and whichever one he chose, he couldn't help but think of her laughing, and then going, *Aww!*, or going *Aww!* and then laughing. And, if they were there, showing the letter to her friends. And then he tried thinking of another answer, that she would have to respond to differently, but she hadn't put *4 Other (please state)* or even left space for that.

He turned the letter over, and sketched in the rest of her body carelessly, then, not carelessly but suddenly solemn, tore up the letter and scattered the pieces over his plate.

THE PEOPLE SEEM SO SMALL AND FAR AWAY

Marion bought Peter a ride in a hot air balloon for their forty-seventh birthday.

'Will we be able to see over the side?' he said.

'We're not that small,' she said.

The pilot did a double-take as they arrived. 'You're—'

'Very alike,' said Peter. 'We're brother and sister.'

'Twins,' said Marion, and Peter scowled.

'You know how that freaks them out,' he hissed, as they clambered in.

It took a long time for Peter to overcome his fear. In that time, while he sat feeling travelsick in the bottom of the basket, the pilot gave Marion his spiel about ballooning, how it worked and what to look for. The 'whole experience'. 'Why not put your hand on her bum too,' said Peter to himself, but he had to admit that, at their age, the pilot probably wasn't bothered. It was all just the same glib patter — and Marion lapped it up, ooh-ing and aah-ing at every sight the pilot pointed out.

In the end Peter realised he was starting to look like a bit of a dipstick, and hauled himself up to the lip of the basket, next to Marion. 'Wow,' he said, and Marion smiled.

'Yes, wow,' she said.

When the burner was on, they had to yell to make themselves heard, and then when it went off, they found themselves whispering.

'Look at that line down there,' said Peter. 'It looks like a massive arm.'

'You mean the canal?'

'No, next to the canal. In that field — beans, is it?'

'Sweetcorn.'

'There's a double line cut in it, where the tractor went. But look, there at the end, it goes all wiggly like a hand.'

Marion did the yelpy-snorty laugh that always put men off. 'Yes — and at the other end — that big pond's a head!'

They were going up, and as they panned out they saw more and more pictures in the land. A woman giving birth. A sow. A monkey-dog. As they watched, a train emerged from the tunnel which was the sow's mouth and Marion shuddered. 'I thought it was a serpent,' she whispered, gripping the wicker lip. She was slightly slurring her words. 'The devil again, spoiling it all.'

There was writing, too. The houses' gables and conservatories and sheds spelt out a blocky font. 'What does it say?' said Marion.

Peter peered. '*Youth, gods, shamma la mam, oh lovers*. No. *You, the gods, shall immolate above us*. It's a sign.'

'Yes. But what about him?' She nodded towards the pilot,

busy pulling a cord to trim the vents.

'He is the Paraclete,' he said, and Marion giggled. 'Shall we do it?'

'Yes,' she said, and they held each other's hands for a long time before Marion opened her bag to take out the implements.

AS GOD INTENDED

My dad's workmates called him the Bear. It was this big industrial area. You came off the main road after the retail park, and turned up past this car wash place. Then warehouses, mostly empty. When you got to the gates you had to cross a big expanse of empty concrete, with weeds growing up from the cracks, to get to the site office. Behind the site office was the works itself, with the diggers and chimneys and so on. But Dad was based in the office (which was really a set of portakabins) and his job was to look after the parts of the site that weren't being used. There were acres of dirt and hardcore piled up in dunes, and bits of scrubland with little whippy birches and scratchy undergrowth.

Every day Dad would go out and find a quiet spot to have a shit. Usually he hid down in the hollow of a dune or behind a bush, but once someone saw him from the Scunny train and made a complaint, and he had to go in the chemical toilet at the side of the office for a week or two.

He told me he never shat in the same place twice. That it was liberating to take his ease in the open air, crouching over a tussock getting an eyeful of page three, then using the paper to wipe his arse. Every day, regular as clockwork. Al fresco. 'As God intended,' he said, and all the lads laughed. It was kind of heroic.

Then one day I saw on the local news a girl had been attacked down there. They didn't say exactly, they said 'an industrial area near the river', but I recognised the skyline and the slope of the ditch. She was 'confused' and wandering on the site, and a man came up and attacked her. They didn't say what, but—you know. Straight away, I thought of Dad. And I couldn't stop.

I went round to his flat, but he wasn't there, so I cleaned up a bit and went out to Aldi to stock up. Then I sat watching the telly and drinking cans. I had this feeling like someone had slit my guts open. I didn't know if I should call the police. He had a stock of pornos on the shelf. I had a look at a few—nothing illegal, nothing brutal, but it made me feel sick.

On Sunday night I was vegging out to Countryfile when I heard the door go. He came in and saw me, and a shifty look came over his face.

'Where've you been,' I said. 'Good week at work, last week?'

He passed his hand over his forehead and scalp, smoothing down hair that wasn't out of place. He paused, and then spoke in a tired voice, 'I wasn't at work last week. I was—on a golf holiday in Dublin.'

'You hate golf.'

He sat down on the arm of the sofa. 'Well, it was the lads wanted me to go. They were going anyway. And, there's this woman. I don't even like her really. But she'd been on at me to go and see her, and everything here had been kind of grim. So I went.

'The thing is, son, it was alright at first. Sex and that. Trying out the local. It's been bad weather over there and all the town was dark and wet and inviting. Reading the local paper and not knowing the places. I really liked it. But.

'I was lying in that bed, a woman's bed smelling of soap

19

and that, looking up through the skylight at the rain, feeling really happy, when suddenly I had the strangest feeling that I was about to die. I just knew it, I felt it. I felt like I was going to die, in the next few hours, last night or today. I don't know if I feel like it any more. It seems daft. But—anyway. I came home.'

WHY THE RENAISSANCE
BEGAN IN ITALY

When Neville had the choking incident I was dead cool-headed. 'I'm not first-aid trained,' I said, and rang down to reception. By the time Burger Rob had turned up and started whacking him on the back, Neville was decidedly not with it. The ambulance arrived and he was still unconscious. Even though they got the blockage out, the paramedics said he had to go to hospital.

After they'd gone I was about to get on with my work, when I noticed his sandwich for the first time, the one he'd choked on. I mean really looked at it, thinking, what sort of food was it lodged halfway down his lung? I wondered if there are taste buds down there, if Neville could taste the thing that was killing him. And naturally that piqued my curiosity and I opened it up.

Thin ham and frilly leaves and mayonnaise and olives. Typical Neville. But what struck me as I stared at the cut side of the bread was how the big the holes were. It was one of those individual ciabattas, and although they're quite chewy when you eat them, I noticed now what an open texture it had—big air bubbles in the dough that opened on to other bubbles, merging together to let air and pockets of mayonnaise seep down into the depths of the bread. I thought of it as a kind of bready foam, and then I thought it was like con-stellations, but instead of stars in empty space you had these planets of space arranged in a universe of bread.

I was peering into Neville's sandwich at the mayo and bits of olive and fragments of ham and frisée when I saw a little grain, down at the bottom towards the crust. Hello, I thought, he's had black pepper as well, but something about it wasn't quite right. So I grabbed the magnifier from the drawer and looked more closely. Bingo—it wasn't pepper at all, it had a little roof: it was a tiny house with granite walls and a steeply-pitched, red-tiled roof. The roof had a dormer, and from the angle the house was lying in the bread I could just about see in through the open window. And the sound—I could hear a very faint noise like two steel wires moving across each other.

It was a violin, a man with a long beard playing a violin, lying back in an ornate wooden chair and playing the violin with a sweetly melancholy air, legs crossed and the top leg waggling in time to the music wearing a long, thin Turkish slipper in purple velvet, decked out with gold thread and little letters in a language I didn't understand. And behind the man against the far wall was an ancient chest, dark like ebony and carven all over with these weird figures, ele-phants and fish and soldiers wearing funny hats, and the lid of the chest was thrown back and inside it were piles of I thought bottle tops but then I realised old coins, and jewels: pink chalcedony, and sapphire, and blue chalcedony, and amethyst.

SITTING ON THE BANK
OF A MIGHTY RIVER

The staff nurse is checking Paula's eyes for a nervous tic when she calls everyone over:

'Look, these blood vessels, do you recognise the shape? It's the Ganges. Paula's eye is a globe showing the Ganges delta!'

We don't believe it at first; this kind of thing happens all the time. It's that herbal tea she uses. Last year she bandaged the water cooler and had to be restrained in the back office. But gradually people kick back from their desks and go over, and there's a swell of excitement round Paula's cubicle. She's staring up into the striplights, and even from here I can see her eyes glistening with unshed tears.

Across the office there's a grid of discarded headsets and another of flashing screens that indicates a network of irate customers holding for longer than they should.

The throng of excited chatter is still growing around Paula, the staff nurse controlling her exhibit like an impresario. But one of the work experience spods has snuck back to his desk and pulled up Google Images.

'It's not the Ganges,' he shouts out in the surprisingly loud voice which shy people are capable of when no one's looking at them. 'It's the Irrawaddy.'

The room goes quiet and they all turn and look at him.

'Strictly the Ay-ey-arwady,' he falters.

For a second no one moves, and then the deputy manager peers over at the screen and nods. 'He's right. It's the Irrawaddy.'

They disperse as quickly as they gathered, taking up their headsets with sour faces and slumping back into their chairs. The staff nurse stands by her charge for a moment, and then goes off to wash her hands, slamming the door behind her. The blind rattles in the gust of air. Paula's left there, her eyes still wide and swivelling, feet clasped together on the chair's base. I can't say anything now—it'll seem like sympathy. But I'm aching to. Maybe I'll follow her out at ten to five and say it in the lift. How I would stare into her eyes whatever the river.

THE WONDERFUL THING

Lilian had three children, all girls, and then a fourth, a boy called Michael, who died a few hours after he was born.

No words can convey the bitterness of her grief in those first days. It covered her. But—she had three other children to dress and feed, and her husband Bunny to share her solitude. So weeks went by, and months, and the grief began to seem like something she could live with.

The months went by until the day of Michael's birth and death came round again; and the grief came back to her in a dark wave. She sent the eldest girl off in charge of the other two. She made a pot of tea and let it go cold on the kitchen table, where she sat, staring at the grain, until Bunny came home.

He hung up his hat and she said, 'I haven't made any dinner, I'm sorry.'

He stroked his moustache and looked at her. Tears were pricking at her eyes, but would not come. Bunny came and stood over her and took her in his arms. He did not ask her what the matter was, and she did not know whether he knew; at any rate he accepted her. She could not say the words, so none were spoken.

Again the wave receded with the days, and Lilian survived. But now all year a gloom lay over her, because she knew that the grief would come again the next year on the anniversary of Michael's death. And so it did.

For five years, for six, for seven, the grief of that day and the agony of knowing it would come spoiled Lilian's life; and when the grief came it was not milder, but came every time in the same dark wave that she thought would drown her. After all this time she could not speak of it to Bunny; she could not pay him so badly for his love. But after the seventh year she went to tell the doctor about her trouble, how the grief came back each year, so strong, and that she could not bear it.

'Give it time,' said the doctor, looking at her across the desk. He was one of the old sort of doctor: he had known her twenty years; they sent each other Christmas cards; he generally went to the golf club but had been known to pop into The Ship for a scotch and soda. 'Give it time,' he said. 'Something will happen. Something will happen and one year the anniversary of the boy's death will come and you won't even notice it.'

The sun was shining as she stepped out on to the pavement and walked down towards the chemist to pick up her prescription. She was smiling. 'Something wonderful is going to happen,' she whispered in her heart.

This year was different. Although she knew the grief would come (it was too much to hope that the wonderful thing should happen straight away), now it was not endless, its return was not inevitable as the seasons. The grief would come, and the grief would come; but one year it would not. Something wonderful would happen and the grief would end; and the thought of that was enough to sustain her through the months of waiting. And then the grief did come, as she knew it must; and it was very hard, as it always was, clogging her throat. But this time the dark wave did not cover her completely, because she knew about the wonderful thing that was going to happen and change her grief.

The years went on. Her daughters grew up, married, moved away or stayed; and she had grandchildren. Fifteen more times the grief she waited for arrived, in all its depthless bitterness. She bore it though it was very hard, because she knew that time would end it eventually.

One spring she was washing up and watching Bunny tidying up the greenhouse for another summer, when he staggered and fell. She ran outside, her heart thumping in her chest. The doctor came and confirmed that he was dead. Her daughters came, one by one, the nearest first and then those further away. They comforted her; there was a funeral; they stayed; they comforted, until their comfort was a kind of irritation. Gently, she sent them away, and lived quietly in the empty house, looking at Bunny's chair and his hat hung up in the hall. She did not go to The Ship, but sat sullenly drinking the cocoa she had taken to, staring disdainfully at *The Price is Right*. She lived silently and alone a long time, apart from on Sundays when her eldest daughter would come with the grandchildren and she would allow them to cheer her. And one evening after they had gone she sat down again in the quiet, at the kitchen table, and fell to thinking about the date, and realised that the anniversary of Michael's birth and death had passed, and she had not noticed it.

BACK IN A JIFFY

I cross my legs. This is hard enough. If I go, when I come back she'll be gone.

It's a chicken salad — rather good, but we don't gorge ourselves. 'No point,' she says, and I don't feel like it either.

'You've been so good to me, Martin,' she says, over the apple pie and custard. If I'd known there was pudding, I'd have nipped out after the main course. 'Standing up for me. Coming here. All for a neighbour.'

'More than a neighbour,' I say. It sounds like comic scolding. I kick myself.

'You'll be glad to see the back of me.'

I wince. 'You know that's not true. I'd never . . .' I'm hardly speaking; breathing the words. She smiles that little closed-off smile. I want to try again, but don't. Don't be selfish, I tell myself. I look at the door. Too much local coffee.

'Somewhere to get to?' I realise my foot's tapping. 'Time to be off then.' One of the discreet Swiss shimmers forward. He's got a tray, and on the tray –

I'm desperate. I can see the clouds falling in her eyes. I want to talk to her, to stop her, but the pain in my crotch is winning. Swallow it, I tell myself. She is.

We clear our throats. She says something which I don't hear, then takes the little cup with the tablets in it. It's going to happen. I think I've started to go and suddenly I think if I've got a dark spot in my trousers then to hell with it. 'Don't do it Linda love please I love you and I'll look after you but hold on I've got to go out for a minute don't kill yourself till I get back,' I say all in one breath and run to the door.

It wrong-foots her. I honestly think if I hadn't had to go it wouldn't have stopped her. But she was interested, then. It hooked her. And that was — what? — six years ago now, wasn't it love?

Go on, talk to her. She can hear us, but she can't respond.

NAMES OF CAKES

He was doing coffee and a cake in every country on Earth. He'd studied the quirky adventure trade and thought he could get a book out of it. There was a nominated charity.

He started in Hull with a Nescafé and a slab of fruit-cake — not bad, really. Then over the North Sea to Holland for poffertjes, Brussels for something fabulous with cream and custard which he ate with a tiny fork, thinking about Poirot's ostrich-egg head, and down through France for numerous excellent *café au laits* in artisan patisseries that shook and clogged his heart.

Vienna was a particular highlight. There he decided to head East through Asia, before doubling back for Africa and the New World. In Greece and Turkey the coffee got stronger and came in smaller cups; the pastries became rich bullets soaked in honey and rosewater. And so he rolled his increasingly portly way to the Central Asian steppes.

Uzbekistan was a country of which he knew little. But already he had been here three months. He'd lost his luggage, and hadn't updated his blog since Georgia.

Most of the local girls kept themselves to themselves. But Nila had challenged him to chess that first day at the café next to Tashkent station, and they'd gone to bed later that afternoon. They did not need language to communicate. The cakes she brought him lacked names, and indeed distinguishing characteristics, but they were sweet and the coffee was coffee.

She was trying to get him a job as a security guard at the factory where she worked as a cleaner. It was possible she was pregnant. They lay in bed at dawn, chattering to one another in uncalibrated voices, licking and sucking each other's bodies with tender urgency. He had a feeling this was the last country he would be visiting.

CALL OF DUTY

I clear the bunker with a grenade and then jump down and empty my clip into the trench. I'm just about to reload when I hear Mum calling:

'Come and say goodbye to your gran. She's going.'

I take the landing quickly, checking behind the doors for gooks, then spin round and cover the stairs. They're clear. I take them three at a time as always, and as always I'm halfway to thinking something about the bobbly wallpaper but reach the bottom with a thump before it gets into words. There's Gran, already in her coat. For a minute I picture a red dot on her wrinkly forehead.

'Spending all your time up there,' she tuts, holding up her face for me to kiss. 'Got a job yet?'

Mum steps in. 'He's on a training course.'

'Again?' Gran thinks I'm just a shrinking violet. 'What about a bloody job?'

'It's difficult for him, isn't it Neil?' says Mum, 'You know that.'

'I made a spoon last week,' I say. 'A proper metal one.'

Gran looks me up and down. That's stopped her. 'Most lads your age prefer knives,' she says, and Mum looks all cross and pleased at the same time.

'You'll miss your bus, Pam,' she says. Mum's harder than

any daft game.   *
   'I love you, Gran,' I say.
   'Yes,' says Gran, and goes.

CICHLIDS

John thought I should have a hobby. After the disappointment of not having children. Something to think about. I couldn't face going out to work.

It's in the lounge on a trestle table. Every day I come down and make a second cup of Gold Blend while John's getting his stuff together. I sit and smile up at him, and then I hear the door go and I feel free.

The fishtank came cheap off Ebay. It's not huge — thirty inches — enough for a small community tank. Tetras, barbs, a couple of loaches. I like to watch them swimming, the way they hang there, shift their relative positions. The platinum tetras are like flashes of metal, a constellation. They all face the same way. It must be something to do with the current. It comes from a little filter unit on the left-hand side.

Some days I never get out of my dressing gown. Just sit and watch all day. It's the shapes. The female dwarf rainbowfish are like miniature kukris. The Gurkha knife. I was proud of that. It enlarges your vocabulary. It's very calming, but then the fish are very calm. The biggest one is a pearl gourami which clicks like a dolphin every now and then. It's magnificent, that small noise, in the cul-de-sac's silence. There's an ugly catfish I never see. But my favourites are the cichlids.

At the moment I've got a lush pair of Apistogrammas.

Yellow and black with bright orange extremities. They lurk around, patrolling, and bully the other fish. They've got these big frowns in their lantern jaws. King and queen of the tank. Sometimes they fall out and he chases her under the arch and round in a figure of eight. He puffs out all his fins like a peacock. He's my beautiful boy.

The last lot were German rams, pulsating blue. Really pulsating. You'll think that's an exaggeration, but they really do. The colour comes from inside. That's one way you know they're healthy. When they're poorly the colour fades and they doze in the corner, all drab and unattractive. When the rams died their bodies were almost white. Even the cat turned its nose up.

Today John gets back around six. I hear the door go, and the rustle of him putting up his coat. I smooth down my hair as the door opens. He comes in and stands there huffing. A piece of balsa cracks under his foot. He waves his hand in irritation. 'When are you going to finish that damn boat?'

THE FLIGHT

Brenda's child is coming early, and she's stuck on the island. I'm going there to help her. I got the call at 4 a.m. and we were on the helicopter by ten to five. Me with my bag of kit. I thank my stars we told that film crew where to go.

The sky is getting lighter but the sun won't be up for another hour. The sea's grey-blue is lightening too. I watch the tiny riffle of the waves scudding under us, and hope we're not too late. Steve is away on the rigs so she's alone up there. The neighbours have been rung but even if their boat's not out on a trip we'll get there before them.

I wish I'd made her come to the mainland when her blood pressure got so high. But it'll be fine. She's strong, and placid. I think of her pacing that white kitchen, with the radio on, and the kettle, and probably a cake in the oven too. I got a shrink-wrapped roll from a petrol station on the way. Waking up to all that neon. And noise, even at that time of night. Tankers, their engines straining at the load as they roared past hookers going home.

I've got such clean hands. I'll make it right for her. What joy she has ahead of her if I can save her child. She isn't my type: a little broad in the face, no pique to push against. Janis would laugh at me, and not feel threatened, if I told her. And it's just how my tiredness expresses itself, but as we speed over the water I can't help wishing I was coming home.

OL' BLUE EYES

My friendship with Aftab survived the first time he took my eye out with a squash ball, but not the second. It meant the end of our Monday-night game, for one thing; and what else was there?

Much later I used to pop in to the office to say hello. People are very kind, but then it's easy to be kind when you're not culpable. I'd go to Aftab's desk and stand and feel the silence of him creeping away, and think, *My game.*

Sitting there with a bandage over your face you have a lot of time to think. The counsellor had told me to embrace the new me. So when the woman from prosthetics asked me what I wanted, I told her. It costs money to make glass eyes that look like squash balls, but I had my insurance payout. Both blue-dots, of course. I rolled the old hazel down the corridor and listened.

They said it would disturb the general public to see a man with squash balls instead of eyes. And so it proved. Mothers especially can get very angry. But there are lots of ways to look at things, and I'm the one who's gone blind.

MUSTELIDS

I've culled mink along rivers in Oxfordshire and Gloucester-shire. I despise the ferret as a a mere pet, but watched proper polecats playing in the dust in Aquitaine. I've followed a weasel up the road, an elongated mouse leaping like spurts from a fountain, till it hid in a chink in the wall, and watched me go past, totally not bothered by the dog.

I sat for sixteen hours in a freezing puddle behind a wattle hide. At 4 a.m., first light, the mother stoat poked her head out of the den and disappeared again. Five minutes later she came out, with four babies trotting along behind her. I held my breath and thanked the earth.

I saw an otter swimming up a drainage ditch in broad daylight. Badger-wise, I've been very lucky. One time I sat in a conservatory in suburban Kent and watched a huge boar digging for worms. We drank Blue Nun and chomped pistachio nuts, and then at half-eleven Bill Oddie turned up, and spoiled everything. Egregious twat.

The pine marten was the first mustelid I ever saw, one Christmas in the 1970s. We followed these little double-diamond tracks through the snow, and suddenly there it was in a tree. It faced us defiantly for a second and then was gone into the dusk. That stayed with me. It's why I do all this, I suppose.

And now I'm out in the snow again. Northern Russia, the taiga. I came to find the big one, *Bulo bulo*, the wolverine. A miniature bear, but more ferocious than a bear. Majestic. It's almost invisible. It's been known to kill an adult moose. It leaps on to its prey's back and bites its throat out, and that's what it's doing to me now.

A GLIMPSE OF THE GLAMPERS

Adrian and Terri were closed to us, at first. We were in the bottom field next to a family from Kettering who played frisbee all day and sat out, drinking and burning sausages, half the night. We tramped up with our towels and toothbrushes to the toilet block, and looked enviously at the door of the little hut. It was open a crack and inside you could see mattresses, walking sticks, the edge of a table. 'We could be in there,' I said, bitterly. 'We've been in Waitrose, we've got books.'

As dusk fell they would come out and sit at their private picnic table, reading under the smug glow of a paraffin lamp. They shared a bottle of rosé — 'Rosé!' I said. 'They must have a fridge in there.'

Jaqcui got suspicious. 'You've been peering at that hut as if it's a pair of tits,' she said, as we lay in the dark with the rain drumming on the tent. 'You fancy her, don't you?'

But it wasn't that. I had to admit that Terri was an attractive woman. But it was more what she represented. Who I wanted Jacqui to be, rather than Terri herself.

I woke early and set off through the dew for a piss and a shave. When I got there, who should be standing at the urinals but Adrian. And I couldn't help but see, him being turned towards me, showing me almost, he had the most enormous cock.

Well, that's depressing and par for the course, I thought. He grinned. I was so cross that I actually pointed to it with my finger and said, 'Big cock, posh hut to sleep in, fit wife. It's alright for some.'

At first I thought he was going to hit me. Then laugh. And then what actually happened was he burst into tears.

It was only a little hut. And there was no funny business — it's not like that at all. We'd spent the day talking, and walking, like diplomats, I felt, round a nearby lake. We'd gone for ice creams, but Adrian and Terri plumped for sorbets. It was hard, that day, out in the open, till night fell. Then we all snuggled up in our sleeping bags, with the lamp hanging from a hook in the ceiling, they opened a good bottle of pinot noir and we taught them how to play Trivial Pursuit.

PARTNERS

Even at night all these whites stay visible. Summer's here, so it's not cold. The smell of the ground permeates through all the cracks and sweetens the pong of the changing room. Even at a county side, everything's rickety.

Statistically we're very prone to depression. They say it's worse for openers. All that time standing at slip, having to be ready. Thinking and not thinking. On hold. The opposition captain might declare at any moment, so you need to be in the right frame of mind, switch on like *that*. Ready to face a swinging ball, homing in on your off-stump, then teasing away from you. When you see it move, you have to hold your line, not go after it. That's what an opener does, wait for something to begin, then not let something happen. My life, an essay in temptation.

Rhian threw me out last night, before we'd eaten. She'd still cooked tea so I must have fluffed it. She stood having words, all small and angry. I blocked each spat phrase then cleared my head for the next delivery. I felt relief at first, like the release of being out after a scrappy thirty. Then straight away going over it in my head: what could I have done different?

We're playing Notts tomorrow, so I came straight here and changed into my whites. After a shock like that. Need to get

42

my head ready. But it isn't helping.

The security light flicks on outside the window. I hear footsteps, cautious. The rattle of a door, and then another. Breathing.

It's Rhian. She stands in the doorway looking down at me, her head tilted to one side. She'd never make a batsman. Oh, Steve, she says, and I know what she means. I sit there thinking Sorry.

She comes towards me, arms twitching to embrace me. Wait, I say, I've got an idea, and go over to the box of spares and start rummaging. She watches me with a strange expression. I hold up a pad and say, Let's meet halfway? and she takes a long time but eventually smiles.

It's not just pads, it's arm-guards, thigh-guards, back-protector, gloves. We miss out the box. The smallest shirt we can find's too big but it really suits her.

We're standing in a clumsy cuddle like two batsmen who've collided half-way down the pitch. Normally you'd each run down one side of the wicket and just smile with your eyes as you pass. Or punch gloves after a boundary, whatever. Maybe that's where I've been going wrong.

Now we're lying in a tangle, two white spiders. The grilles on our helmets clash when we try to kiss, the pads and guards keep our bodies from really touching, but I've never felt closer. We must look like angels.

THE PRISONER OF MANSFIELD

It took years of manoeuvring, but I finally whittled my duties down to the licensing of ice-cream vans in the Mansfield area. Mostly I would be truculent, a jobsworth. They usually gave in pretty quickly. But sometimes I'd try another tack. Swapping offices was a good one. That's how I ended up in what had been the cleaners' cupboard.

You'd be surprised how many ice-cream vans operate around here. It's not a front for organised crime, though. It's all about selling ice cream. The best pitches take years to come up; and when they do, it's a simple matter to re-allocate them. Titchfield Park — that's Molinari's. Fisher Lane — Capitto's. The Mr Frosty franchise runs Forest Town and out to Rainworth. I've got it all set out on a special map.

Some people would feel the lack of a window, but I don't mind. I get my meals from the canteen, or Cerys brings me something off the trolley. Bless her. I used to nip out to the Four Seasons, to WH Smith's and Topman, but nowadays I just order my stuff off the internet. I get my washing done internally too.

The divorce was amicable. I have an idea she was called Ianthe, but that seems unlikely. Once a year on our anniversary I pop out to Softees in the marketplace and buy a mivvi in her honour.

The nights are best. I've been reading these Gothic novels—Radcliff, Lewis, *The Castle of Otranto*. I got shivers with *Melmoth the Wanderer*. Bram Stoker. I don't like the newer stuff so much, not enough cobwebs. *The Turn of the Screw*. I sit and read, going for it, listening to the clanking of the town hall pipes.

THE BEST OF FATHERS

A fledgling in a nest, that's me. Except I never fledged. Why would I, when Dad brings home such treasures, all for me? White Lightning, cigs, kebabs. Smellies from Boots, tweezers, toothpicks. E45. Spandex, woolly tops. And even knickers, French stuff, lace, all that—he's brass-plated, him.

Best of all is what he gets from the charity shops: old vinyl, Danielle Steele, a teapot, a tray. A framed repro of 'Sunflowers'—'by Van Gogh,' he says, as if I don't have the telly on all day. He leans it against my wheel while he goes to make a cup of tea. 'Don't use that powdered milk,' I yell, but with Dad it's not if he hears, it's if he listens.

Twenty Berghaus jackets—not for me, but later a silver necklace is. Real diamonds too. He stands and brushes my hair and gives me news and weather. Lattes from the Starbucks which has opened in the old laundrette. 'Dad, do you ever . . .' I say, but his look stops me. A hat. A bowl. A dog. A vintage Singer and some thread. Some photographs with people in them. Money.

One day a dildo. 'New,' he says. I say, 'No,' and give it to the dog. The next day he comes back from Age UK with an awkward boy. Quite pretty, though. We stare. Dad locks the door, a hammer's shank sticking out of the pocket of his trackie bottoms. 'I'll be upstairs,' he says.

LAPTOPS

She sits down in the last seat of the Norwich train out of Piccadilly and puts her laptop next to mine.

'I'm a Mac,' she smiles, and our eyes meet.

'I'm a PC,' I smile back.

'So . . . What does that mean for *us*?' she asks, and the train starts moving.

'It means you're sassy, probably in new media and too fit for me.'

'*Fit*?' she frowns. 'That's a very Microsoft word.'

'But *sassy*'s Apple.'

She looks me up and down. 'You might be right. Here, have a look at this.' She opens the Dashboard and a little widget shows our geographical position.

'And this,' I say, selecting a new theme for Windows 7.

'And this,' switching to split screen, half Tiger, half Leopard.

'And this.'

She stares. 'Wow. I thought the train wifi blocked that kind of thing.'

'It's on the hard drive,' I say, my heart thudding. She leans her head in to see. She seems impressed. I can smell her hair.

'Would you mind turning that off?' says a woman standing in the aisle. 'It's offensive. There are children present.'

I open my mouth to answer but the Sassy One closes the screen on my laptop and says quickly, 'Let's get off at Edale and get a room at the Cheshire Cheese.'

'OK,' I grin.

I never thought it could happen. As we lie there afterwards I suddenly say, 'What if you get pregnant?'

'If it's a boy, we'll call it Linus,' she says. 'If it's a girl, Eunice.'

MARKINGITIS

I had a lot of marking that semester. In the summer we were going to Bangladesh, and I'd taken on extra teaching for the money. But I couldn't settle to it. It wasn't that the scripts were bad: second-year criminology. I'd seen a lot worse. Their referencing was excellent. But me and marking are like magnets with the poles aligned: we repel each other. It's as if my arse is allergic to the chair.

We had these wonderful plums from the hippy shop down the road, really special. They shone with light, or whatever. So juicy. My girlfriend had gone mad and bought us a boxful. They were sitting there on the kitchen table — so I made a little rule.

If I got the end of a script and I hadn't had a plum, that was a first. It indicated sustained attention. If I'd had one, a two-one; two, a two-two; and so on. If the essay couldn't keep my mind off the plums, it couldn't be any good.

It was a good system: when it went for second marking I didn't get any queries. The external examiner praised us, and I like to think the plums did their bit. But I hadn't reckoned on the consequences: I shat brown water for three days.

When we realised what it was we called it *markingitis*, a bad dose of comfort fruit, and that was that. A giggle. But after we got to Bangladesh my girlfriend came down with the shits herself. It happens: different food, different water. We said it was markingitis again, and maybe it was the heat but we thought it was inordinately funny. She'd sit there in the cubicle of our chalet thingy, shaking with laughter and shitting, while I made cracks about the students being responsible for this, about plum bum and fruit juice. And so on.

She couldn't keep much down, but she was game, and kept up a dry chuckle at my gags. I had a look round the neighbourhood and came back with stories and a few bland treats. And always the markingitis jollity. It was really pretty funny.

On the sixth day I came back in with a glass of coconut milk and asked her if the exam board was sitting that morning. She didn't even smirk. I went over and found her skin felt all clammy.

She never regained consciousness. I had to call her parents and tell them. It was a sad time, of course, and I didn't mention markingitis on the phone or at the funeral in England later. They were dignified and polite, and I was grateful to them for that. But even now, when I see a bowl of plums, I can't help but smile.

THE BLINDS

The man and his son stood by the window. The man was talking about the books in the bookcase, occasionally pointing to one or running his finger along its spine. He was wearing his new jumper. The venetian blind was down, and the man could not see the cold night outside.

But his son was half his height, and the slats of the blind angled down towards his eyes and not away from them. Although he tried to listen to what his daddy was saying—lovely Daddy, talking in his nice voice—through the window he could see a bright half-circle of moon, and more bright stars than he could count. He had never seen anything so magical. He didn't know why Daddy wasn't talking about them.

BOLLOCKIN BOLLOCKS

The boy sat putting his shoes on in front of the gas fire. The sofa was brown with pink roses, and felt worn and scratchy when he put his hand on it. A radio was on in the kitchen, and the noise of a newsreader's voice, but not the words, hummed through to where they sat.

Dad and Nana were playing cards at a table behind the sofa. Next to each was a glass and a can of Vaux light ale. There was a plate of crackers spread with cream cheese and a jar of pickled onions. They weren't talking, much: there was the flick and snap of cards being played, and the occasional low laugh or murmur that the boy didn't catch. Or Nana would pick up her cards and say, 'Bollockin bollocks,' under her breath, and the boy and his dad would look over at each other and smile. Nana smelt of parma violets.

He stood up and put on his anorak and danced through the kitchen where tomorrow's weather was the same as yesterday and today. He left by the side door and got his bike that was leaning in the passage, and pushed it up the path and on to the road.

The houses of the estate were made of dark red brick. The air was cold and smelt of the sea like it always did. He rode round the back of the club and down the back road towards the cut-through that led to the rec. He knew she was going to the pictures with her friends but would call in for chips on the way, and this would take them across the rec, and that was where he'd talk to her. He relived the smile he'd shared with his dad and wheeled the pedals backwards in his confidence. She'd laughed at what he said in Geography yesterday. Her dark hair was just right for him.

He stopped at the bollards. She was sitting on the wall at the far end of the cut-through, laughing again. Simmo was standing in front of her, sort of between her legs. Simmo was two years above them.

He watched them, breathing shallowly through his mouth. He couldn't compete with those big hands. She was swinging her calves and flicking her hair back and looking up at Simmo, now laughing and now perfectly serious.

All he wanted to do was talk to her and smell her hair and maybe give her a tiny clean kiss, but that was not what Simmo wanted. The more you were asking the more you were offering, it seemed like. 'Bollockin bollocks,' he said to himself, turned the bike round and rode, weaving through dogshits as he went.

YOU CAN CLOSE YOUR HEART BUT I CAN STILL HURT YOU

Lucille had changed the locks, so I went back to the van and started mixing a batch of mortar. She'd been on at me for months about repointing the house, so by God why not do it now.

It had been in a bad way for years. We'd concentrated on the inside, adding the en-suite and converting the loft, putting in that laminate flooring she liked so much, and then re-doing the kitchen. We were never very garden people, so we hardly looked at the outside. One day when I was measuring up for the conservatory I noticed the mortar had started to go. But I had my hands full, what with the conservatory and everybody in Bolton having stuff done because they couldn't afford to move, so I let it slide.

At first I tried to think of things I could put in the mix to piss her off. Loud pigment. Dog shit. Too much sand, so it would flake off in a week. But then I thought the best thing was to play it straight, so I made up a batch as good as any I ever did, got the ladder up, and set to work.

I knew she was at her sister's till Thursday. On the second day I nearly brought Neil to make sure we got it done, but then I thought, No, this is one job I'll do alone. I stood there halfway up the side of the house — *our* house — grimly grinding out the old mortar, then smoothing in the new, and one minute I was thinking, This'll show her, this'll freak her out, and the next, Maybe she'll ring, at the weekend. To say thanks.

DINGHYHEAD

Philip's condition had a long name, but we never bothered to learn it. He was just Dinghyhead, and he could hang around when we played footie on the bottom playing field, as long as he didn't try to join in. After all, he was excused Games.

His mum worked at a warehouse and he got Refresher lollies by the boxful. His sister was fit, but she was a member of the Christian Union. One day in the summer he took off his trainer and showed us how all the toes on his foot had fused into one, with five little islands of toenail strung across it. He said it was an 'archipelago', and then he told us about this amazing book.

It was funny how in the holidays we were drawn to the place we loathed being in the rest of the time. The empty buildings felt sinister: drab blocks of classrooms with big windows, and service roads and sports halls and caretaker's sheds. It was a warm, dull August, with clouds covering the sky and the air stinking of dogshit and privet. We stood by the goalposts and looked up at the labs where chemicals waited under lock and key; and under them the offices with sarcastic women with flowers on their skirts and filing cabinets and in the filing cabinets pieces of paper with lists of our names. On top of the kitchens was a chimney with no smoke coming out and on the very top of the Humanities block was a big aerial or radio mast, and we talked about what it was for, but none of us knew.

That gave us an idea, and we skirted the field and tramped down through the woods and over the beck to listen to the air at the substation. 'What can you hear, Dinghyhead?' we said, for a bit, and then Miller told him to climb over the fence, but he said, No, he was deformed, not an imbecile. So Miller hit him. He just turned round and walked off, with Miller stood in a cloud of midges shouting, 'Yeah, go on, fuck off!', a line of spit flinging out from his mouth on to his own shoe and the big leaves of the nettles.

I caught him up outside the launderette and walked with him for a bit. I had a silver-plated cigarette case in my pocket that had been my grandad's. It was warm from where I'd been holding it in my hand, but I hadn't shown it to anyone all day. I took it out and told him about the metal smell on the inside. We talked—well, I did—about his sister, and the Battle of Britain. I asked him if he wanted to come back to mine for tea.

'No thanks,' he said.

WHAT IS AND WHAT
SHOULD NEVER BE

Sometimes a word just sticks, the noise of it at first. Then you
see it everywhere. What it means.

I'm like that with *akimbo*. I was stood like that, hands
on hips, watching the louts smashing the glass in the bus
shelter, and I thought, 'That's a strange one'. *Akimbo*.

Soon it wasn't just arms. Two dogs faced each other akimbo
in the park. I noticed that the sycamore outside the library
was quite definitely akimbo in the splay of its branches. I
forgot about it, then Ned walked back from the bar, pints
akimbo, and that set me off again. 'Have you ever thought
about . . .' I said, and of course the answer was No.

Back at the flat the postman had been and at the far end of
our correspondence British Gas faced me, bills akimbo. The
Yellow Pages had been leaned up by the doorstep and I realised *akimbo* wasn't enough. So I had a go myself: The Yellow
Pages leaned galimba against the wall. Easy.

Why stop there?

Changing the light bulb I observed that the lampshade
which hung sharidny from the ceiling had a slight dent. I
stood bungla in the kitchen while the kettle boiled, the mug
waiting tastar on the side.

Cabataxl. Diddid. Flake. Eratus. I compiled a physical

lexicon, but saw that it had no end. No one was interested, not even Ned, and so I was just making stupid noises with my mouth. New, but stupid. That's how you go mad, isn't it?

Then, walking istwards back from the pub one night I glanced in to the windows of the community college and saw her. All my words, and more—it was a semaphore class.

I hadn't paid any fees, so I had to stay outside in the rain, but other than that I was just another one of her bunglers, watching her say things with her body. All that time I'd thought I wanted the words for shapes, but she gave me the shapes for what I wanted to say. And that calm, mathematical dancing helped me see what I wanted to say, too.

One night I followed her home and saw her use new words, new letters she hadn't taught the others. The way she leaned against a lamppost waiting for the cash machine. The peck of her finger on the keypad. I don't know how to write what she said, but I understood her. And after she had gone I watched other people in the street and suddenly understood them too. They used, or tried to use, her language.

This is the last class. I'll miss her. I know she's not been speaking to me in particular. But as I stand bulbecular in the flowerbed, she turns to me and smiles, and before she turns off the light she spells out G-O-O-D-L-U-C-K with her eloquent limbs.

ORANGINA OR APPLETISE

Bryony put the phone down and found herself floating to the living room. She did a little pirouette in the doorway, humming the love song from the latest production of the Tamworth Players. Fi's daughter had had the baby, and it was called Fleur.

'*Fleur?*' said Brian, who didn't approve of modern names. 'Sounds like a flower. In fact it *is* a flower. French, isn't it?'

Bryony raised her eyebrows, but Brian wasn't looking. His gaze was fixed on the television screen. He waggled the Wii remote in the air like a disembodied penis.

'It's not a name I can get my tongue around, and I'm not alone. It sounds like Schloer—you know, that new soft drink. Elderflower flavour. They don't put enough sugar in. Here, Fleur, have some Schloer.'

Bryony had been going to tell him what Fi had said about the builder Brian drank with, but thought better of it. The glare of the screen lit up his face, but in a sinister way. 'What's wrong with Orangina or Appletise, if you want a posh soft drink?' he asked. Bryony thought of the chest freezer in the garage, which had a box of Oranginas on top of it next to the bread sticks, as surely as if Brian had led her there by the hand. 'Ridiculous,' he added.

Brian was always touchy when he was losing to Federer.

Bryony walked back into the kitchen. As soon as she did so Fi popped back into her head. That was happening a lot recently. Cheeky Fi, sitting there in her airy house saying charming things, being attractive to attractive men and annoying the hell out of Brian. Sometimes in the shower or doing the ironing in an empty house Bryony found herself murmuring *What would Fi say?* out loud. She picked up the phone.

'Hello?' Fi's voice sounded like a smile, and Bryony could hear herself half laughing already.

'Hi Fi, it's me. Listen. I've got an idea for the summer farce. Wait till you hear it. It's called 'Sex with a Ghost'. Twisting the phone cord round her fingers. Waiting for Fi to respond.

NEXT DOOR TO MURDER

Exhausted, we slept through until five, when Paul got up for a wee and saw the blue lights flashing in the grey of before-dawn. He stood at the window looking out, and when he started scratching his bollocks I knew he was thinking so I got up too.

There were three squad cars blocking the street bang outside our house, and an ambulance too. The street was taped off and five or six police officers were stationed around, keeping onlookers out. More were moving to and fro, talking into radios and writing in notebooks. In the houses opposite were the faces of our neighbours, watching like us as the drama unfolded.

'What's happened?' I said, shivering and linked my arms through Paul's. He'd stopped scratching his nuts.

'Summat's happened next door,' he said, and he was right: the policemen and women were concentrated in next door's garden, and every so often one of them would go in or come out, and talk to the others and walk off up the street.

It was exciting for twenty minutes and then we got bored, and we were just getting back into bed when the doorbell went. So Paul stuck some pyjama bottoms on and clumped downstairs. I lay there listening but I couldn't hear anything so I went downstairs myself, and there was Paul stood in the hall talking to a dark-haired WPC.

'No, we didn't notice anything,' he was saying. 'No, we didn't hear anything. Nothing at all. Otherwise we would have . . .'

She was pretending not to notice the stiffy that was half-awake in his pyjamas. She looked up at me coming down the stairs and our eyes met. 'Sorry,' I said, and put my arm round Paul's waist.

After she'd gone we went back up into bed and allowed the stiffy to develop. It was gentle, unusual sex, with the birds beginning to sing and the muted voices of the emergency services coming through the window. Then we lay breathing deeply and Paul told me that the WPC hadn't given much away. 'But it sounded serious,' he said.

'Mmm,' I smiled into his chest hair. 'Yes. Serious.'

After breakfast I negotiated the cordon and headed off to work. When I got back, the street was open but a police van and two squad cars remained, and next door's garden was very much under occupation.

'It's murder,' said Paul flush-faced as he handed me a glass of fino. 'I had a word with Audrey oppposite this afternoon. He killed her in the night. Don't know how. But it was messy.' I must have raised my eyebrows. 'A murderous rage,' he added. Then: 'That's the SOCO's van. It's just arrived.'

I won't go into our gossip and excitement and fevered speculation — it's too embarrassing. But later, after we'd eaten a half-shoulder of lamb and watched Blue Planet on the box, we headed off for an early night. Paul hung back in the doorway of the bedroom.

'Thing is,' he said, and gestured at the wall. I frowned. 'SOCO's still in there,' he hissed.

'So?'

'They'll hear us.'

'It isn't *our* fault,' I said. 'It's not like we're in mourning. Life goes on.'

'Well . . . OK,' he said, and started getting into the suit.

MATTHEW

Holly Wragg was the first. She'd been a regular in my pilates class but dropped out, and then a few months later turned up at the door with a pram.

'He's yours,' she said.

I couldn't believe it, and nor could my wife. 'I never touched her,' I said, and after I'd said it a lot of times she started to believe me.

'But you *thought* about it,' she said.

I said, 'Well . . . '

Because there was no doubt about it. Holly Wragg was a pretty girl.

The next was a couple of weeks later—Gemma Smith, from my form at school. I hadn't seen her in years, although I'd had a massive crush on her way back when. So it was a shock to have her standing on my doorstep with a teenager that had my eyes. I heard my wife sigh and tut behind me in the hall.

After that it was a steady stream. I was the daddy of the street. There were a few celebrities—Abi Titmuss, Dame Kelly Holmes, the one off *Live from Studio Five* that's not Jayne Middlemiss. But mainly it was women I'd met at work, in the pub, passed gawping in the street. One or two of them I didn't even remember. All these kids I didn't know I had. For a while I was actually pretty pleased—but then I wanted it to stop.

The wife went through a series of emotions: anger, disbelief, dejection, jealousy, and finally acceptance. 'You didn't touch those girls, did you?' she said.

'No,' I said, with the righteousness of he who speaks the truth.

When Gill next door turned up waving the two lines of the test kit under our noses, she just turned to me and said, 'I thought you said she looked like a grumpy horse,' as if I'd forgotten to mow the lawn. We were getting through it.

But then one day Holly Wragg knocked on the door again. The pram's handle rested on the bulge in her belly. I watched my wife working out the dates.

'You didn't,' she said. 'After all we talked about, you couldn't help yourself.'

'Look,' I said, 'It's a very proud moment, becoming a dad. It draws you closer to the mother. It's hard-wired. It's chemical. And when you asked me if I'd thought about it, I couldn't help thinking about it again.'

A LONG, LONG TIME

Felix and Leona had disagreed about the space mission from the beginning. It had never blown up in a full-scale quarrel, but Leona let her feeling be known about the whole business: the risk, the disruption, the time away. 'It's my job,' said Felix, and the simple way he said it seemed to foreclose further discussion. Leona would go away and bang pots, or make a phone call to the PTA, using her irritation in the pursuit of others, and later they would make up, really make up, opening their hearts to share the love that was the reason this whole thing mattered, and have some pretty good sex too.

Felix really didn't have any choice, so he went on with the training. He was preparing his body and especially his mind for the opportunity he had been looking forward to since he was eight years old. It was important to know how the mind would behave in space, how to control that behaviour and build the correct habits of thought.

Sometimes the preparation meant staying late. He would come home in the dark and Denzil would already have cleaned his teeth and got into his pyjamas, and Felix would sit with him for a few minutes and Leona would come in and stand in the doorway watching them with a face that said, 'This look has softened because I love you and I know you love your son, but I have not forgotten my anger either.'

Finally the day came when the space mission would begin. The astronauts had all been given a week off with their families, since the mission would take six months and for much of that time they wouldn't even be able to talk to each other on the radio. Felix and Leona had taken Denzil down to the coast, eating at Jimmy's every night and playing on the beach during the day. Leona had known Jimmy at college and he was just this goofball who had plenty of money and ran this guesthouse on the side. Most nights it was just the three of them, snuggled up on the verandah, with Jimmy strolling up with a handful of beers and a cold milk for Denzil. In all that week Leona and Felix hadn't talked about the mission at all, but on the last night he had given her a necklace and she had given him a new watch and although he couldn't take the watch up into space because of regulations he had been overcome with love and gratitude, and known that it would be OK.

In the family room they said their goodbyes like the other families. Everybody was tearful, except Leona who had gone quiet and kept her arm round Denzil the whole time. Just as they were going, when in fact Leona and Denzil were already halfway through the door, Leona turned her son round and said to him,

'Look, take a good look at your daddy. He's going away for half a year, which is a long time, and you won't see him at all, and it's because he wants to go and play astronauts like all the other boys. But he's thirty-seven and he should know better.' And she stepped forward and pushed the door to so that Felix couldn't see Denzil and said in a low voice, 'It's OK, we'll stay at Jimmy's. See you when you get back,' and then she too was behind the door and the door clicked shut.

Felix thought of all the preparation and training he had

been doing on mindfulness and controlling his thoughts. He wasn't so sure that he could control them, but he knew with complete certainty what he would be feeling and thinking about for the next six months. And the one spark of joy in his brain was the humble acknowledgement that he had not won the argument after all.

AMUSE-BOUCHE

Mostly I work the farm on my own, driving over from Inverness, bombing along the empty roads and down to the water's edge by daybreak. When my son can get a day off he'll maybe turn up too, but a night in Glasgow's better than a day in the oyster-beds. Even I know that. Anyway, I like the emptiness.

This morning it's low tide, and I fix up the Landrover to haul one of the cages to a better position away from the main current of the loch. It's the cold that makes your hands clumsy. Pain and not-pain. I don't mind that. The equipment's heavy, too heavy for one really, but I have a job to do and I do it.

I pour a cup of bovril from the flask and stand staring at the far shore thinking about my sons. It's nothing but sky above heather and grass and grey stone above freezing water. And the rocks at your feet. High in the sky I see a bird wheeling. I'll say it was a sea eagle, and maybe it is.

The tide's coming back in and the sand's softening with the water. I finish the job. I've got to move the Landrover up above the high water mark. Don't want it getting stuck again. I start to uncouple the chain from the tow bar. The clasp's clogged with sand and salt and it won't come open. I get some oil from the back and douse it, but it won't budge.

The water's lapping at the tyres now. I fetch a crowbar,

lever it under and use my other hand to hold it in place while I yank it. I pull at it and pull at it; it gives suddenly, and I fall back. There's a pain in my hand. I flail in the shallow water and my hand stings ferociously. On my feet again, I look down and see it's taken off my little finger.

There's not so much blood as I would have expected. Maybe that's the cold. A thought strikes me, and I look about wildly for the finger. There it is, caught in a strip of seaweed. I grab it and stride out of the water.

Up on the shore there's a hut where I keep some tools. There's a brazier in there somewhere. I lug it out, throw in some scraps of wood and light it. I'm conscious of shock and the cold. I wrap a clean rag round my hand, then hold up my finger in the other hand and look at it. I think of wrapping it up as well, but I'm worried I'll lose it so I keep holding it up like a candle. All this cold and salt must be good. I can't get it any cleaner, or colder.

After a while I lay the finger on the lid of an old biscuit tin and stand and watch the sea swallowing the Landrover. I'm stuck here till a boat comes past on the loch. It could be hours. I'll set off the airhorn and wave. Even then it'll be an hour round the loch to the main road, and two hours to the hospital at Fort William. I try to remember how long a limb can survive detached from its body.

The finger is dull and going duller. The hand is livid underneath the rag. I try a tentative waggle of the remainder. It makes the wound hurt but they move. That's something.

About midday I start to get hungry. My piece is on the passenger seat, wrapped up in a square of grease-proof paper. I remember there's a quarter-bottle of Scotch in the hut. It's probably too late for the shock but I dig it out and slug it anyway. There are gulls above the loch now, calling and turning. A small plane crosses a corner of the sky.

I'm pretty hungry. I look at the finger on its field of tartan, an extra stick of shortbread. An idea strikes me.

Before I know what I am doing, I pick up the finger and lodge it in the dying embers of the brazier. There's a bit of smoke; it smells acrid. I watch as the skin blackens and bubbles, and take another slug of whisky.

When it seems done I reach in and pick it out quickly, then drop it back on the lid of the tin. That's wrong, isn't it, raw meat and cooked meat on the same board? It sits there, cooling. I reach down and pick it up, then try a nibble between the knuckles.

I suppose it does taste a bit like chicken; not much eating on a finger, so it's hard to tell. I use my teeth and tongue to strip away the flesh, and then there doesn't seem much point in keeping the bone, so I hurl it into the loch. The taste, both pleasant and unpleasant, lingers in my mouth. A barbecue. I wonder what I'll tell my wife.

THE HARBOUR WALL

'Jilly asked me something funny today', said Julia, staring out of the window into the bay. This was their fourth night, and the cottage was starting to feel familiar. Comfy. Ross appeared in the doorway with his toothbrush in his mouth and made a noise which meant, 'Continue.'

'How did they build the harbour wall? Actually she said, "Did frogmen build the harbour wall?" and that's as good an idea as any.'

On the way back in Ross tossed a paperback on the bed. 'Maybe they did it at low tide.'

Julia stopped brushing her hair and shook her head. 'It's never out that far. Remember? The base of the wall was under water all afternoon. That Welsh bloke never stopped fishing. Do my aftersun?'

Ross was a good masseur. Julia felt the cool of the lotion against the day's warmth in her skin. He worked at the muscles in her shoulders.

'And anyway the tide would come in and wash away the cement.'

'Quick-drying? Special cement that dries underwater?'

She wrinkled her nose as she turned and lay back on the bed. 'Nowadays, yes. But not in the old days. When was the harbour built?'

Ross kissed her and looked out of the window. The sea was calm and almost inaudible. The last of the light was fading across the sky. 'A long time ago. Except that doesn't seem to be possible.'

She reached round and grabbed his buttock. 'So it must all be a sham. The harbour wall was built after the invention of special underwater cement—'

'By frogmen—' He laid his hand on her stomach and made a gentle circling motion.

'By frogmen. Evidence that the world is much younger than we think. In fact underwater cement is no use. How would they transport it *before* they'd built working harbours? The whole of history is a fabrication.'

He reached down lower. 'What about other people? Older people—like our parents.'

She rolled her eyes. 'Robots.'

'Clearly. The world was created just before we were born, so they must be robots.'

His fingers had found their usual spot. They were quiet for a while. Their breathing came in slow, comfortable waves. Then Ross looked up. His fingers paused. 'But if that's true for us, it's true for Jilly.'

Julia looked at him with a quizzical expression.

'The world's a set-up, right? So one day Jilly'll have this conversation. And she'll come to the same conclusion—sauce for the gander. So, that proves we're robots. You and me—we're robots.'

A small amount of smoke rose from Julia's ear.

THE VARIATION

The door opens and she's there—about my age, shy looking. Not dreamy, I hope. There's a lot of it about in my line of work. 'Miranda?'

'Yes,' she smiles, and in spite of my tight shoes I smile too.

'I'm Susie.' Behind her there's a leafy pot plant, a smell of joss sticks. She opens the door wider and I go inside. We stand in the hall, all polished wood, but gloomy, dark in the middle of the afternoon. The ticking of a long-case clock.

'It's in there,' she says, and ushers me into a sitting room full of junk. Not junk—expensive, old: a Persian rug, mirrors, vases, little tables piled with little things. And in the corner by the grate, where a fire is just beginning to catch, the harp. That smile of a whale.

It needs a clean. 'I haven't touched it,' she says. *You're all apology*, I think. It's nothing special—nice, but tatty, and not old enough. Still, I reach my hands round it to embrace its air, breath in its dust. The curve of the neck seduces me: I reach out and stroke it, then feel the flakes of gilding crumble in my fingers.

'It was my grandmother's,' she says. I turn round with a jolt; I'd half forgotten her. 'The whole house, in fact.'

'It's very . . .'

'Yes. You're like her—photographs, I mean. That red hair.'

75

She's getting talkative. 'She lived here all her life. Did you see the orchard in the lane?'

I blush. 'I took an apple, actually. For later. In my bag.' I turn to rummage.

'Oh!' she laughs. 'I didn't know. I wasn't . . . You're welcome to it. Would you like a cup of tea?'

And though I don't want to I feel I must say yes. While she's gone I sit down at the harp and lose myself. I see the patches which her grandmother's arms have worn, the tiny drifts of grime and dust—her finger ends—at the joins and pins. A few notes, and it doesn't sound so bad; not bad at all. I play.

She comes back in; I stop. She looks about to gush so I break in, 'A rather lovely harp. Not worth a lot, as these things go. I could find a home for it, but I think it's at home here. It's nice to play—'

'So play,' she says, and again I find I can't say no. So I take a sip of the tea she has set down beside me and think *To hell with it,* and embark on the *Variation de la Reine du jour.*

It feels good to be playing an old harp, and without an audience, or hardly one that matters. My ear, inside that sound, my mind. I play a long time before I think of her at all, and then I look over and she's lying back on her grandmother's chesterfield with her eyes closed and a kind of ecstatic look on her face. Wow, I think, Go for it. And the thought of all the pleasure that I'm bringing her—memories, too—makes me feel better too, and on I play. And as I play the feeling is intense, the sense not just of music but of being in this room, the light which falls across the room's victoriana from the window, the peaceful silence of the house. I play, and somehow my legs are feeling rather weak. Miranda's still with her eyes closed on the sofa, breathing slow and heavily, and sometimes she seems to make a quiet hum of appreciation.

I play for a long time before I notice she's got her hand down the front of her jeans.

And when I do, for some reason I don't stop, but carry on, and smile to myself and turn away, towards the fire which is warming my right leg and arm. My scalp tightens; my hair is standing on end. I stare into the flames until the cadenza comes to its close, then look out across the room, but not at her, as the last notes resonate beyond their end. I feel extraordinarily calm. When I look over she's looking at me, both hands now on her lap.

'Thank you,' she says. I sit tight. The ticking of the clock in the hall. 'I hope you didn't mind—'

'Oh no,' I say. 'It's fine.'

'It's not you,' she says. 'Although, the hair — it helps. Relaxes me, or something. Is that weird?'

'Yes,' I say, but in a friendly way, and we both laugh. I clear my throat. 'Actually I found it rather beautiful,' I say, and blush for what she might think I mean.

'I'm glad,' she says, and there's a cadence of finality in that phrase that tells me it's going to be alright. I gulp the cooled tea and check my watch.

'Will you come again?' she asks as she sees me out.

I take the apple from my bag and step through the door into the day. 'Oh yes,' I say.

GARETH

My son became a tramp in 1992. Neil Kinnock and John Major barking away on the telly meant nothing to me. Our beautiful boy was sliding away and we couldn't help him. One day I turned up at his flat, already exhausted by what was to come, and he'd been evicted. And that was it. No fixed abode, ever since, not that I've known of.

There were a few sightings in the early years. Little Keith Lee from the garage saw him in Keighley in the summer of '94. We laughed about that in the car on the way up — Keith Lee in Keighley. But when we got there, nothing. Four nights in a dingy B&B, trawling the streets and the parks and the off-licences. Nothing.

Then one year we got a call from the Royal Worcester Hospital. He'd been taken in. By the time we got there he'd been discharged. We looked around, and went back when the shift that had seen him came back on. They remembered, but they couldn't tell us much; he was a tramp. Alcoholic, tired, been about a bit — but doing OK. Alive. Cheerful. Irascible. It sounded like Gareth, and yet not Gareth. Done in. A shadow.

And that was it. We never heard of him again. I like to think of him down here in the south-west. It has a certain timelessness; somewhere to lose yourself. When I say 'He's dead to me,' people think I'm angry. But he's free of us, of everything.

He's got that freedom you get when your parents die and we still got to go on living. Eileen sixteen years, me more. He's on no lists. I think of him moving along: all those stories, all that alcohol. His swearing and violence. His mighty suffering. Heroic — not Superman, more Odysseus. He stepped aside and made his own world. I'm not saying he's happy.

There's so much tiredness between us. That's the only thing that keeps us together. I bought the campervan after Eileen died, sold the bungalow and came down here. I'm not hoping to find him; just to be here, nodding to his friends. It's no way for an old man to live, on the road. Every couple of days going to the cash-and-carry. Here, take another bottle for when you wake up. You'll need it.

THE COLONEL'S
EXECUTION

On the morning of the colonel's execution we asked him if he wanted anything as a last request.

'Yes,' he said, 'a couple of bottles of whisky. Three. To be on the safe side.'

'He wants to drink himself unconscious,' Max whispered to me behind his hand, 'to save himself the terror. We'll have to sit him on a chair.'

But it wasn't as simple as that.

He sat at a table and drank. We took it in turns to sit with him, and of course at first he was taciturn and then, as the alcohol took effect, loquacious. He told us the story of his life in disjointed anecdotes, and we lay out in the field outside the farm, smoking, and piecing them together. It almost got that we felt funny about shooting him.

As the first bottle ended and the second began he talked more and more about the last years of his childhood and the first of his army career. 'That summer I spent working at the cement factory,' he said slowly, staring at me with those bloodshot eyes, 'was the happiest of my life. We walked to work through the woods and got drunk in the evenings with the girls we'd grown up with. Do you know—' and he described to me at length the girl who he had remained in love with his whole life: her sharp tongue born of shyness, his own incompetence, their walk alone down to the riverbank and their one kiss, somehow never repeated in spite of his gawky ardour.

He slugged back another glassful of the whisky and grew morose. I left him, and five minutes later I heard him laughing again. He was getting garbled, his mind sliding around, always coming back to that summer, that girl and the friends of those days.

He did not need balancing on a chair: he was conscious to the end. But when they brought him out from the barn, leaving behind the table and the empty bottles, his walk had the loose-jointed stagger of the very drunk. He was talking, still, under his breath, and I strained to hear what he was saying to us. But then I caught her name, and I realised he wasn't talking to us at all. His eyes swept my face without a flicker of response. They led him off, and we followed, towards the appointed spot. He was not walking through the farm, but through a wood, and not to his execution but to another meeting on that riverbank, another kiss. And we were sending him to paradise.

MEETING IN THE MITTEL

Jonah's fiancée broke it off and went back to Wigan, so Jonah chucked his job and got on the Eurostar. He'd always wanted a city break. So there he was, sitting on the balcony of a boutique hotel in Vienna, in a baroque street off Der Graben. He could see the crowns of passers-by's heads, hairy whorls that danced along from university to opera house as they had done for a century.

He was waiting for the waiter to bring his schnitzel. But there was no hurry. He had begun with a glass of pastis, and whiled away an hour or more over a small platter of cold meats that he ordered as an afterthought. Then a liver dumpling soup. He had dribbled a few drops when eating it; but since he had a huge starched napkin tucked into his collar, the white suit he had picked up in Marks was unblemished.

Later he would have coffee and a strudel. He had a copy of yesterday's *Times* and would make a show of reading it. But more interesting was a cloth-bound copy of Hofmannsthal lying on the empty seat next to him, which he thought he could manage with the aid of the German-English dictionary secreted in his breast pocket.

The waiter brought his schnitzel and set it down in front of him, then neatly refilled his glass with the wine he had picked at random from the middle of the list. He shot his cuffs and picked up his knife and fork, but just as he was about to set to he felt a sharp pain at his wrist. An ugly yellow fly had bitten him. He flicked it off and watched it disappear in a swirl above the ceaseless heads. Where it had bitten him there was a tiny red mark, and it began to throb steadily.

That throb blunted the pleasure of his balcony lunch, but only slightly. He abandoned the *Times* as an affectation and had a go at the Hofmannsthal. In the time it took his coffee to go cold he faltered to the end of a single poem. He wrote it out on a sheet of paper that the waiter brought him. It wasn't a bad translation: a man and a woman meeting, he on a horse, she carrying a flask of wine. Some of the phrasing seemed to him rather good.

Later he strolled through the streets, and drank a couple of brandies in a neon-lit bar. But the bite on his wrist was bothering him, and he went back to the hotel to sleep off the train journey. Tomorrow he would press on into the old empire's provinces.

He fell deeply asleep very quickly, and that was good. But after a few hours his sleep became shallower; he moved his limbs restlessly and unconsciously scratched at his arm. And suddenly he found himself in a monstrous dream—walking down the corridors of a lurching ship, unable to find the open air—and soon came face to face with a huge insect that filled the bulkhead door.

At this scale its hairiness was more noticeable. The yellow cast of its skin was phenomenal, virtually custard. They eyed each other for a moment, and then the creature spoke:

'I am the fly that bit you this afternoon. There's blood between us.'

'Yes,' he nodded vigorously, urging it to go on.

'Europe is getting rather dangerous for us. I know about your important work. The best thing for us is to travel far

away. I'm thinking of Central America. We can talk and
play backgammon on the way. I'll help you improve your
German'—here the fly made a lop-sided face which seemed
to indicate a jocular dig—'and you can order me the meals I
desire. We are one, you and I.'

'But how . . .'

'I shall be your secretary. Once I had a home in the moun-
tains. No one will suspect anything. Later, once the voyage
has settled down into a delicious monotony, I shall come to
your cabin at night and we shall attempt sexual union.'

DR SCOPOLI

It is an open secret that the material they extract from the quarry damages the men's health. In twenty years there will be lawsuits, but this is a time and a place where they don't complain. And if they do, no one listens. 'Why would they?' says Franco, sitting on a deckchair in front of a line of washing. 'They hardly bother about my children going to school. I can hardly feed them. Who is the government going to listen to, me or the company, whose directors go to dinner with ministers?'

They visit Dr Scopoli most afternoons, shuffling diffidently into his consulting room in their work clothes. He sees the dust that comes off them on to the examining couch, into the air he breathes. They have pale faces and little niggling coughs. He frowns into their throats, eyes, ears, scratches his temples. He doesn't know what it is. But he is worried. He writes harmless prescriptions and they go away pleased. He telephones his friends at the university, in the ministry (but it is the wrong ministry), at the squash club. They are friendly, would like to help, make small promises. After he has put down the receiver he looks at the pot plants in the corner of his consulting room and waits.

In the evening he puts on his jacket and cycles round the hillside to his home on the edge of town. He kisses his wife, whose knee is troubling her again, and takes up his children in his arms. They eat, in the last of the sun, and he tells her he is worried. She listens, but she has heard it all before. Afterwards she does the dishes, gets in the washing, while he plays with the children in the yard.

CHESTNUTS

Carol has never been able to make any of the men in her life understand about horses. They tend to think of it as a hobby, like tennis, or just ignore it. The one time she tried to explain about the aching, the guy thought she wanted to have sex with a horse. Or possibly on a horse. Either way, he was prepared to think about it. But that isn't it at all.

So now, with Rob, she's cautious. She drops a few hints, and leaves it at that. She makes out that he wouldn't understand. Reverse psychology.

'Very brown, your horse,' he says one day, on the way back from the stables. 'Shiny brown, deep brown, very very deep brown like a really well polished table.'

'That's it!' she says, and then wishes she hadn't broken cover. They're quiet for a while.

'Or like a conker,' he says, having thought about it. 'I could stare at a conker for hours.'

She feels a bit sick. This is it. She gives it a go. 'That's how I am with horses. Staring at them. The sheen of the brown. But' — challenging him — 'not just the look of them. There's the smell. And the feel of them, the feeling you have on your hand and in your heart when you stroke a horse's skin. Not so much the head, but the rump or the flank.'

He frowns slightly, or is that the evening sunlight making

him squint? She's put him off, she thinks. He's quiet, turning the car down the narrow lanes. Then he pulls up in front of a five-bar gate. He strokes his stubbly chin. She waits.

'Well,' he says, faltering at first. 'That's like a conker too. The feel of it in your hand. Smooth, and then the velvetiness of the light bit. The hardness, the not-quite-a-ball digging in your palm. Or in your pocket, digging in to your thigh. A pocket full of conkers is as big a treasure as I've ever owned.'

She's smiling foolishly. 'And the smell?'

'Oh . . .' He gestures, confidently now. 'The smell of leather? They don't smell of leather, but I feel like they should. Or the smell of pockets. I'm sure conkers have a distinctive smell. Even if I can't think of it.'

They laugh.

'Do you—' she doesn't know why she's saying this, except she wonders if he's a nutcase, 'do you mean in a sexual way? Would you like to roll conkers down my naked body?'

He looks at her. Neither of them knows where this is going. But—that look they give each other, eyebrows rising. They're not thinking about horses at all.

KEITH AND I

Keith and I drove the wagon for Randall's Beds for seventeen years. We'd pack it with frames and mattresses at the depot at four in the morning, then spend the next day and a half on the road. We made good time, the best, because we took it in turns, and while one was driving to the sound of Radio 2 the other was sleeping in the back on the best mattresses money could buy.

We took particular care with the packing. You had to make sure a premium mattress was accessible. I wouldn't lay a tart on the cheap ones. King-size, quilted, memory foam, organic cotton orthopaedic — owt like that we'd bung in flat at the back. Then round the corner we'd stop and one of us would jump in for forty winks.

It was like a religion. We'd sleep for twelve hours out of thirty-six, then go home to get our heads down. My Cheryl used to go on about health and safety. She thought we must stay up all night, for all the sleeping I did at home. But I couldn't get enough of it.

Best of all was three or four in a stack. You lay on the top and it was Iggle-piggle's boat floating you off to dreamland. The drone of the engine was the churn of the sea. Once I got seasick and chucked up over some bird's small-double Snuggle Tuft.

That night we had a round trip to Oban. We dropped off a brass frame in Burnley and Keith took the first stretch, up the M6 to Kendal. Then we swapped over and I took us up through Dumfries and Galloway and Glasgow. Janice Long was playing the Eurythmics. The motorway was as quiet as it ever was. Keith had had a long pull up from the West Country the day before so I let him be.

When I opened the wagon doors at the Oban showroom to get out these futons for holiday lets I knew straight away something was wrong. Keith had died in his sleep. He was curled up like a big fat shrimp. Poor bugger. I know I should have said something to the security guard who'd let us into the compound. But instead I chucked the futons out as quick as I could, holding my breath, then slammed the door shut and got the hell out.

I stopped in a lay-by down the road and sat with my head in my hands and cried.

THE REGION OF DANGEROUS ROADS

The moorlands of the Dark Peak contain the most dangerous roads in the UK. It's official. There's often fog or ice. They drop suddenly round sharp corners, sashay through hairpins. It's the national limit, with plenty of slowpokes and ditherers to enrage you. And if you do come off, you'll tumble into a boggy valley or meet a drystone wall with an unforgiving crunch.

Further south the geology is different, and the ways between villages cut through steep-sided dales. Everybody speeds except the tractors you meet suddenly round corners. Across the top of the plateaux the A-roads are white with limestone dust. You sway out to overtake a Tarmac lorry into the path of a BMW.

Screetham Lane is a narrow rat run down from Matlock Moor to Beeley. Wayside twigs scratch paintwork. A pheasant gets it. The Calver road's full of battered saloons of boys with pockets full of draw and speed, converging on an empty house where Dan will tell us he found a injured sheep and killed it with a rock.

Then there's the track that leads to the farm where I'm going to meet Leila Thompson. There's her pale blue eyes, the dog barking on the end of its chain, the cold, her slender figure that makes me feel lucky and hopeless, and her farmer father watching from the back of the unlit barn.

BANJO PLAYERS

Any situation is improved by the presence of a banjo player. For example: at a funeral, that twangy merriness inspires a healthy acceptance of death, and makes the wake more lively. *First day at school? Uh, I know a song about that . . .* And so on.

I'm talking about the finger-picking ones, not the ones who strum it like a guitar. The banjo player is a kind of specialist clown, halfway between jester and Jesus. He takes on the futility of all things, sucks it in with that long-necked hoover whose sound-box is as vast as the spaces of America. And the listeners are left free to move across the futile ground, ordering a beer or expressing their love or laying down the law (banjos are particularly good in court, if the judge is liberal enough to allow it). The businessman closing a deal can point to the dude tapping his foot in the corner and say, *At least I'm not like that guy.* And the up-tempo music makes the clients smile and sign.

At a wedding the best banjo player makes everyone get lucky except himself. He is at length accompanied by the creak of bedsprings, the banjo's wire cousins. He keeps on playing; it is his gift to the world.

But perhaps he is weak, or a girl stands mesmerised by his dancing fingers. Then it's over. Because a banjo player with a family is something else. You see a photograph of a man on a cart. He has a grey beard and a paunch, and there's a banjo on his knee. He's smiling, and you know he's playing a happy tune. But next to him is his wife, and on her knee two toothy redneck kids. All smiling. And this time the futility of which he speaks is not pleased at such mockery. It takes a clawhammer to your heart.

TRAINING A CHAMPION

Luton were away at Plymouth and Carl's lift let him down, so instead he took Ryan out into the park for a kickaround. He was so happy, holding on to his dad's hand, with that simple happiness that shines out of their little faces. The door clapped to and suddenly the noise of the fan in the oven was the loudest thing. I was glad to see them go.

It couldn't last. The cake was cooling on the side when they came in. Ryan toddled over to his jigsaws and started chewing on an edge-piece. Carl slung his jacket over the bannisters and slumped on the sofa with a face like a heavy home defeat.

I knew right away how it was, but no, he had to tell me. 'Can't even kick the bleedin thing. Can't hardly hold it, even.'

'He's only two, love,' I said.

'Sid's kid's three and he can take penalties. They do these little give-and-goes round the sand-pit.'

'It'll come,' I said, handing him a Carling.

'It *won't*. You know as well as I do it's a matter of aptitude.' And he turned on Sky Sports, using Mr Chucklestonks as a cushion. Ryan watched him.

After a while of Carl watching the telly Ryan got bored, and came to ask for a glass of milk. I gave him a slice of cake with it. The icing wasn't set yet, and it smeared round his face and made it shine again.

When he had finished I gave him another, and had one myself. We sat at the kitchen table in the quiet, grinning at each other with full gobs. 'More,' said Ryan, so I cut him a third slice, as big as the others, and put a glacé cherry on top. I stood at the window smoking a fag while he ate it. If Carl's going to despise him anyway, I thought, to hell with it, why shouldn't he be my special little fatty?

SMOKING FOR RUDD

A rudd's like a happy roach. See how it smiles. And this is why.

Rob's granddad took him out before the dawn, down in his old Micra to the mill ponds. As it got lighter they could see mist in the valley above the trees and the ruins of Wraggs works. There was a haulage yard at the end of the road. It looked deserted, but Granddad said it wasn't. The rusty containers that said *Maersk* and *China Shipping* on the side would be going somewhere one day soon. But there were dandelions and dock growing up round the edges and through the seams. They could hear a dog barking—a big Alsatian on a chain, Granddad said—but they couldn't see it.

They left the car at the end and crossed a wooden footbridge over a branch of the river. The path opened out into a clearing, very flat and covered with straggly red weeds and daisies and foxgloves. There were patches of bare concrete where the weeds hadn't overtaken yet. Where the slabs met the weeds had gone out along the seam, fat thistles and other spiky growths tethered in a tiny trough of earth. Behind the trees Rob could see a big house with chimneys and many roofs, broken windows and no lights on to show somebody getting up for work. He held his coat tight with his fists in his pockets and hurried along next to Granddad. Granddad was carrying the tackle.

They dropped down to a mesh fence and walked alongside it in silence. One the other side of the fence was the empty works. There were brick buildings with flat roofs and metal doors, covered in old graffiti, spiral staircases in the same metal up the sides of walls and in by the base of the massive chimneys. The chimneys had weeds growing at the top and out of cracks halfway up, and were dribbled in bird shit. The main shell of the works was three levels of open space, held up by concrete pillars. Rusty water sat in pools on the ground floor. There were pieces of machinery, fused into rusty lumps, bolted to the floor; a sluice gate, smelling a bit like the sewage works. They walked alongside the ghostly works for a long time and when they had left it behind went up a flight of stone steps to the bottom pond. The tail goyt was guttering and spewing last night's rain out into the sheer-sided leat in sudden gushes. Rob's stomach rumbled, and he wondered when Granddad would let him eat his sandwiches.

They found a spot and settled down. Rob helped Granddad set up the rods and used some water from the pond to mush up the bread. Granddad had a coughing fit, and Rob could see his old breath floating out and disappearing into the air. It was fully light by now.

'They used to make fire bricks up theer,' said Granddad, jerking his head upstream towards the next works. Rob didn't know why he was telling him that.

They used waggler floats and only a little weight on the line, with a dab of bread on the hook. But Granddad wouldn't cast straight away. He put his rod ready on the rest and searched in the pocket of his long coat for the cigars and a box of matches.

'Shy buggers, rudd,' he explained, getting down on his

hands and knees and then flat on his side across the path, with his head poking over the dull surface of the pond. He lit the cigar in a sudden flare of foul-smelling sulphur and began to chuff busily to get it going. Rob watched him fade into a fog of thick smoke that was almost green. It smelt good after the sulphur. Then Granddad put his cheek right down by the surface and began to exhale the smoke in big, gentle clouds over the water. He did this for a long time. Rob fiddled with a few pieces of gravel he had picked up. The smoke spread slowly out in the still air, covered their side of the pond in a wispy cloud.

When the cigar was done Granddad sat up on his fold-out chair and poured them each a cup of tea from the flask. He stared with far-away eyes at the fug over the water. And smiled.

'Yer have to do that a lot for it to make much distance,' he said. Rob's brows knitted for a moment. After a couple of sips of the hot tea Granddad went on. 'The rudd like it, but they have to — to get addicted, like. But after a while. They take on the habit. It brings 'em up good.' And he picked up his rod and cast.

LEARNING TO
LOVE MR LAMB

The new butcher gave Dave stewing steak instead of fillet, and
that ruined Dave's special meal. So on the Monday he went
back and complained. The butcher looked embarrassed and
bobbed his bald head down behind the packets of parsley
sauce mix, mumbling something which Dave couldn't hear.

'Pardon?' said Dave.

The butcher's shoulder sagged. 'OK,' he said, 'come with
me.' And he took Dave outside and pointed up at the shop's
sign. 'Look.'

MR LAMB, it said, in ludicrous gothic lettering which
matched the smaller writing underneath, *Award-winning
meats and pies*, left over from the time of the previous owner.

'*You* won't be winning any awards,' said Dave.

'No,' said Mr Lamb. 'I only took on the shop because of my
name. It's been a sort of dream, but I haven't trained. It's all
a bit new to me. It's more difficult than I expected.'

Dave felt his stomach rumble. 'Look, I'm a life coach.
You're clearly cowed by an obstacle. And what do we do when
that's the case?'

Mr Lamb's eyes searched Dave's face, his lips working
silently to find the answer. Dave found it for him. 'We eat
the cow.'

The butcher's expression brightened. 'Really?' he said. 'I've got half a cow hanging up in the back.'

Dave steered Mr Lamb back into the shop and past the counter. 'Let's get to work. The only way to learn is to get stuck in. You must construct your own knowledge, not swallow the knowledge of others.'

Mr Lamb was muttering excitedly under his breath. Dave could hear little phrases: 'Flat steaks . . . bad end of scrag . . . minced corner . . . the long bit . . .' He texted Nuala to tell her he'd be late.

They stood before the side of beef in the cold room, their breath clouding in front of them. Fat and flesh covered the surface of the meat in patches, an undiscovered country, veined with estuaries. Mr Lamb pushed open the bar of a fire exit to reveal a boy smoking on the doorstep, and handed him a twenty. 'Take this,' he said. 'We're going to need some mustard.'

A NEW LOOK

When I mix paint for people in the back room it goes in these generic tins, so they don't know until they get it home that I've given them the wrong colour: pillarbox red for magnolia, summer sky for granite, sweet pea for aubergine.

That's just the start. When they come back I put their responses into categories. Replace; Refund; Sent Angry Spouse; and Foul-mouthed Rant—they're the popular ones. Violence or Threat of Violence is also fairly common. I go limp and let them hit me, and they soon stop. But then there's Accepted New Colour with Good Grace; Adultery Resulted; Adultery Suspected by Spouse; Attempted Religious Conversion; Broke Down and Wept; and, more common than you might imagine, Shat in Miscoloured Paint and Poured Over Doorstep of Shop.

But only one customer thought to taste the paint, and discovered that her sandalwood dream was really lobster bisque. She came in yesterday, and that's when I told her she'd won. She was a little surprised at first, but we had a long talk and in the end I think she understood. I leave the shop's premises and all its stock to her, Ellen Sarah Watkins, to dispose of as she sees fit. Tell my dad I'm sorry.

BETTER THAN COD

I can't stop thinking about Hugh Fearnley-Whittingstall. All I ever see is him going on about pollock, how it's better than cod and we should eat it and save the cod stocks.

I'm very happy to, but last Sunday on the book stall I picked up a copy of Rick Stein's *Seafood Cookery*. Fifty pee. Published 1987. And there's the rub. All *he* says about pollock in there is how it's not fit to grace the table and he'll only use it for soup. And they can't both be right, can they?

Does Rick eat pollock now? I could Google it and find out, but that's not the point. He could be as deluded as Hugh. Or maybe Hugh's been right all along, and Rick was just being snobbish. It comes down to fashion. In the 80s nobody had a reason to eat pollock so they didn't rate it. Now the cod's all gone and we've got to learn to like it. It's so confusing.

They're both Gadiformes. It's a hierarchy: cod at the top, then haddock, then whiting, pollock. Hake next, I think. Anyway. It got me thinking. I'm not questioning Hugh's honesty. When he crunches down on a battered pollock he must think it's as heavenly as he says. And if we can't trust ourselves when it comes to fish, what about the other stuff?

I mulled it over all Sunday night and Monday. On Tuesday I was clearing out the cupboard behind the organ when Tara came in with fresh flowers. I explained it to her as best I could. She blushed and didn't really answer. I don't think she understood. We've never hit it off as well since the incident in the vestry.

So I kept it to myself a while longer, till I bumped into Phil tending his mother's grave on the Wednesday. I unburdened myself.

'Reverend,' he said, 'I can't say I've ever hankered to be a Catholic. The robes and that. Have you?'

'It's not the robes,' I said. 'It's having to make do. After Henry the Eighth was excommunicated.'

'Yes.'

'Once your cod population's depleted, you move on to something else. But if cod came back on the menu . . .' I spread my hands and raised my eyebrows in a question. I felt like the devil.

'Not really, no, vicar. Honestly.'

So I had to leave it. But I can't help—last night I found myself browsing the internet for candles. It's a very disturbing thought, finding out I'm aligned with Hugh Fearnley-Whittingstall. An amiable and worthy man, certainly. But I'm not sure he has the authority I'm looking for. I have to be strong for my parishioners, and I'm not sure I can do it now that I know we're pollock. Small fillets, delicate flakes. We're not even haddock.

JUDY

Judy wasn't local: she arrived one day on the high street, marched into Blooming Lovely and asked Karen for a job. Karen had just lost the Saturday girl — she'd gone collecting glasses at the dogtrack. She put down the irises she was cutting and said she'd give Judy a try, but don't come in those great boots tomorrow missus.

Outside the shop was a pelican crossing, and over the road was another florist's, Val's, and on her third morning Judy trooped in saying Val had undercut them on bunches of daffs and cheap sorrys, which is what they called the wilting bunches they put out front in a pot for men to buy their wives when they felt they had to. Karen wasn't rightly bothered, but it did piss her off a bit that Val would do that, since there had always been plenty of business to go round, especially now that the big Interflora up by the pub had closed.

Someone cracked the glass in Val's window on the Saturday night, and the next week Judy started having chips at lunch. Karen wouldn't have minded but the smell was putting the customers off so she had a word with Judy, who sulked for the rest of the day and pushed off at four.

Then Karen came back from the wholesale market one morning and found Judy all red-faced and salty and sticking out her bottom lip. Karen's husband had tried it on with her, she said. Pushing her against the counter. Lost his rag.

'With flat little tits like that!' said Karen's husband when she asked him, 'She's trouble, that one,' so Karen told Judy she had to leave.

Funny thing was, the next week Karen was watering the hanging baskets first thing when she saw Judy clumping around setting up at Val's.

Judy kept herself to herself at Val's and stayed late tidying even though Val said she didn't have to. But then Val found her crying in the back room and Judy said she wouldn't believe some of the stuff that went on over there at Blooming Lovely. Blooming Horrible more like. Nasty Karen and her creepy bloke — and Val should hear some of the stuff they said about *her*. Val made Judy a cup of tea and Judy said if it came to it she would stand up and say those things in court.

At Halloween Judy got some presents for Val's kids. Daft, cheap things, a cape and vampire teeth for Michael and a sexy witch's skirt and top for Rhiannon. Val thought Rhiannon was a bit too young for that but when she said so Judy's face dropped into an awful scowl, and the next day she started telling Val about how this lad had screwed her, in front of the customers and everything. Then she took a two-hour lunch and when she came back she kicked over a display of lilies and shouted effing this and effing that and something about an industrial tribunal.

The next day Karen dropped in with a couple of chocolate eclairs from the baker's and Val made her a mug of Mellow Bird's. Val said, no, we never dropped the price of the bargain bucket, and Karen went fuchsia pink at the thought of all the things she and Phil had apparently got up to. Now Karen and Val go line-dancing together and Judy, who works at a bookie's in Halifax, says they're cows.

A WHITE PEAK PROPHECY

What Lucy loved about the house was the gable-end. It was entirely covered in some sort of ivy and you could see it as you approached through the village. 'Imagine what it'll be like in autumn,' she said. 'I bet it goes bright red or orange. It'll be a work of art, the centrepiece of the village.'

And she was right. We bought the house. I had to stretch the budget a little, but she had her heart set on it.

The locals took to Lucy straight away. She makes friends fine, and living there, making a new home in that picture-postcard village with its white stone walls and green fields, how could she not? She helped with the well-dressing, walked the dog with the woman from the pub, and shopped at the shop. Naturally, they loved her.

I was shyer with them, and they with me. Away most of the week, I didn't get much of a chance to get to know them. But one Friday in October I drove down after my afternoon meeting, and when I turned the corner and saw the house I had to park up and get out, just to stand and look. The ivy had changed colour, as Lucy had said it would. In the evening sun it blazed with fire. I was dumbstruck.

After a moment I noticed a man standing next to me. It was the landlord of the pub, with a docile Alsatian on a lead. He grinned and nodded at the house.

'It's wonderful,' I said.

'A beautiful house for a beautiful woman,' he said, and I smiled at his courteous compliment. A couple of his friends, the builder and the man who ran the farm shop, strolled up behind us and we stood admiring the shining wall in easy silence.

I went in and made love to Lucy and afterwards I told her about how she had been right about the wall, and about the village too, and she smiled like the cat who got the cream, and I kissed her again. I didn't think much more of it till winter had set in.

It was another Friday afternoon. This time I'd managed to get away straight after lunch; I'd been away since the previous week on a trip to sort out our regional office in the south-west. In the time I'd been gone the last of the leaves had fallen from the trees. Again I turned the corner, and I saw that the ivy too had dropped its leaves, or at least they had shrivelled back to the brown stems, leaving the wall barer than I had seen it before. And it turned out that behind the stems a huge cartoon face was painted on the wall.

At first I thought it was a devil. But there was nothing devilish about the expression of that imbecile face. It had a silly smile of anguish, and a tear falling from each of its deathly, circular, pupil-less eyes; and a cow's horn sprouting from the hair above each ear.

I got out of the car, mesmerised by the horrible face. I heard a noise like the chattering of jackdaws behind me, and turned to see the landlord and his two cronies, laughing. They weren't laughing at the face, although they could see it blazoned huge behind me. It was not a humorous laugh. On the contrary it sent a shiver through me. I looked straight at their faces, and their malicious eyes returned my stare without the slightest flicker of embarrassment.

THE WHALES

Ruth checked the numbers on the doors on either side then stepped hurriedly down the passageway into the little court-yard. There was an Italian restaurant on the bottom floor, and the rain beat loudly on the red-and-white umbrellas and the metal chairs stacked against the wall. Shut. The shop was on the floor above. A staircase ran up one of the walls to the door. She could see the faded sign fixed to the brown stone-work: *Desmond Lewis. Curios.*

At the top of the stairs she found the right key on the bunch and opened the door. A bell jangled above her head. A strong smell of damp and — tinsel? — hit her. She stepped inside and smoothed the rain from her hair, pulled off her coat and looked around.

She'd picked up the keys from the old man's solicitors on the way. The local firm, old-fashioned but aspirational, an LCD screen on every desk. Mr Talbot had an iPhone which he'd laid in front of him like a sheriff's badge. He'd asked her about the Gherkin, oyster cards, said something about coming down to catch a show. *To catch a show.* She didn't believe him, but she wasn't sure she was meant to. Those laughing eyes. Friendly, she supposed.

She'd half-expected him to tag along, show her the way to her inheritance, and when he didn't, but palmed her out with a gracious grin, she'd felt slighted, the stranger unwelcomed. But now, breathing the dusty air and standing in a pool of water on the bare floorboards of the shop, she was glad. She would do this alone. It was hers.

The shop covered the whole of the first floor, with a little flat above, and downstairs the restaurant on a different lease. Maybe she could eat there later, if it opened. She rather felt that she didn't care to look at the flat, though she supposed she would have to. It felt intrusive; no one had touched it since her great-uncle had died. That didn't matter in the shop; she even liked the thought of it. But upstairs: half a tube of toothpaste, a ring round the bath, a book by the bed. She did feel sad, a little, that she hadn't known the old man. But how can you love someone if you don't know they exist?

She found the light switch (black bakelite, of course) and flicked it on, then luxuriated in the room's contents. It was as she had dreamed it every night since she got the letter. Snowdrifts, tides, of bric-a-brac. Furniture. Paintings. Jewellery. Crockery. Clocks. Decanters. Medals. Walking sticks. Swords. Boxes — Tunbridgeware, carven, military. Carpets. Enamel advertisements. Glass cabinets. Typewriters. Stuffed animals. Telephones. Retro hoovers. Vinyl. Cribbage boards. Glassware. Edwardian pornography. Model boats. Gasmasks hanging in sombre bunches from the roof. Rails of costumery. Hatstands. A mannequin dressed in a salmon corset and a tricorne. And a door into a second room and beyond that, she knew, another.

She could hear the rain steadily pattering on the windows. The traffic was barely audible back here in the courtyard, even through the old single panes; just the occasional drone as a car flashed past the gap at the end of the passageway. It seemed a sleepy town. Maybe it was half-day closing. She thought they might still do that here.

A boiler came on somewhere nearby and she wondered if it was the restaurant or if the flat's heating had been left on all this time. It seemed an affront to the old man but then she remembered it was hers now and the bill would find its way to her. She put out her hand to the iron radiator and felt it: cold. She wondered if this would damage the stock.

There was so much to know, and she turned to the counter where she had flung her coat and saw the piles of folders that she would have to go through. But not yet. First the indulgence of her proprietorship. She walked slowly through the room, touching things, picking them up, caressing them. She looked around for a *Breakages must be paid for sign*, couldn't find one, and was glad. She noted the prices scribbled in biro on stickers and tags, and knew herself drawn forever beyond the veil between buyer and vendor, that mighty reversal of high and low. A china cat. An inkstand. She stood for a long time holding a photograph of a piano player in a gilt frame. She wandered over to the rails of costumes, reached up to the limbless torso and stroked the material of the corset.

Its touch was wonderful. Silk with a definite nap. Under the silk she could feel the outline of the slats. It was trimmed with white lace, setting off the pinky, browny orange of the silk. Quite beautiful.

She pulled tentatively at the tea chest that lay between her and the mannequin. It scraped along the floor, the oddments that sat on top of it wobbling madly. Then she stepped up to the mannequin and gently untied the ribbons that held the corset shut.

It took her twenty minutes to get it on. She closed the blinds and released a fresh cloud of dust, then quickly undressed to her socks and knickers. It was cold, but she didn't care. She couldn't pull it properly tight, of course, but she got it on and tightened it as best she could, sucking the air and pulling, her arms tangled behind her. The ribbons left white marks on her fingers.

Once it was on she staggered out into the middle of the room in front of the counter. A newborn foal. She caught sight of herself in a tall mirror, but it wasn't about that. She could hardly breath. Her ribs felt bruised, crushed. The edges cut into her and her flesh bulged round them. She felt the intense pain-pleasure-panic-excitement of asphyxiation, and though it had not up until now been sexual, and in large part remained like that, she suddenly understood certain things she had hitherto disdained. She put her hand out on to the back of a Queen Anne chair, reproduction, to steady herself. She groaned, quite loudly, and breathed, 'Oh yeah,' saliva rattling in her throat. 'To hell with the whales.'

NO LONGER COVERED IN THE TRAINING MANUAL

Improved meteorological information meant that it was rare now for an airliner to pass through an electrical storm. So even though Sasmita had three years' experience in cabin crew, when the darkness outside began to flash she got the heebie-jeebies. She scuttled up to the service area and shut the curtain. There was Janie, reapplying her lipstick.

She stroked Sasmita's arm. 'Has it shit you up, duck?'

Sasmita nodded. Her collar had begun to feel uncomfortable.

Over the loudspeaker came Big Daddy's calm baritone, telling the passengers everything was going to be alright. Which it was.

Janie knelt down and pulled open a door at the foot of the bulkhead. Sasmita had always thought vaguely that it contained a dinghy. Instead, squashed up to the corners, an exceptionally tall man to put in such a place, was a priest.

He climbed out of the drawer and adjusted his cassock. He had thick dark hair and a lantern jaw. Sasmita smiled automatically. Janie handed him a miniature Bell's from the trolley.

'Bless you, my child,' he said. 'Bless you, bless you.'

He was stiff from being cooped up like that. Janie helped

him round towards the toilets.

'Is it bad?' he asked.

'It's not good,' said Janie. Her voice was hoarse. The plane was rocking, and lightning lit up the sky every second. Sasmita wiped her hands over the serge material on her buttocks.

Janie reached behind the door to the gents and pulled the end of a cable out from the wall. It was covered in plasticated casing, but the end was metal, a curved tongue roughly the size and shape of a dessert spoon. 'Good luck, Father,' said Janie, and passed the cable to the priest.

He knelt down on the cabin floor, crossed himself, and took the metal tongue in his mouth. He closed his eyes. Janie and Sasmita watched him, holding their breath.

'Is your hair standing up?' asked Janie. Sasmita nodded. 'That's the charge in the air.'

Suddenly the plane was struck. It bucked wildly, but only for a moment, and then settled down again on its former course. The priest half rose to his feet, but Sasmita could see that the movement was involuntary: the muscles of his limbs were contracting as a massive electrical force passed into him. He shook, violently, for three or four seconds, and a smell of roasting lamb filled the air. Sasmita saw his face blush red, then purple. His jaws were working and his temples pulsated.

Then just as suddenly it was over. The spoon dropped from his mouth, and he turned to face them. A small amount of blood lay in the pits of his eyes, as if he had cried it. And his wonderful dark hair was standing up, was salt and pepper, and had tilted him from young Antonio Banderas to middle-period George Clooney. He advanced a step towards them, and raising his trembling arm bawled out, 'οὐχ οὕτως οἱ ἀσεβεῖς, οὐχ οὕτως, ἀλλ᾽ ἢ ὡσεὶ χνοῦς, ὃν ἐκρίπτει ὁ ἄνεμος ἀπὸ προσώπου τῆς γῆς. διὰ τοῦτο οὐκ ἀναστήσονται ἀσεβεῖς ἐν κρίσει, οὐδὲ ἁμαρτωλοὶ ἐν βουλῇ δικαίων· ὅτι γινώσκει Κύριος ὁδὸν δικαίων, καὶ ὁδὸς ἀσεβῶν ἀπολεῖται.'

'Shit, man,' said Sasmita, and got ready to deploy the debilitating gas.

'Don't worry,' said Janie. 'That happens every time.' She helped the priest to sit down on the floor, and made him put his hands, flat together, between his thighs. After a minute or so he fell asleep.

So Sasmita went into the staff toilet to freshen up, and then took out a tray of free chocolate oranges, to distract the passengers. It took a while for her hands to stop shaking. It was funny, how the pith on a real orange was so fiddly, but chocolate oranges got so maddeningly stuck together, through the absence of pith, or perhaps the useless presence of a pith of air.

COMING HOME

She lives in a bungalow on one of the far limbs of the town, but ever since her husband died it doesn't feel like home. Without his warmth, his being there asking for sandwiches, the walls feel thin — no longer reverberating with his voice, just the telly.

So she took this job. She isn't old. She shows people round houses that are empty. She gets the keys off the agents, goes round and turns the heating on, opens a window if it smells, and welcomes the buyers when they arrive. And then they go, and she shuts up again.

Most of the houses are empty, because the owners have already moved. That's why the agents need her. Quite often, the owners have died, and then some of the furniture is still there. Not the best bits. The families must come and take what they want, and leave the rest. A flat-pack cabinet. A wardrobe too big to move. The dead woman's bed.

But this house is nearly full. There are no clothes in the wardrobe, but there is cutlery in the drawers. Most of the furniture is still there. The owners live abroad. When it's sold, they'll put the furniture into storage, but for now, they're saving the expense. She walks around and it feels like somebody's home. Her home.

It's been on the market a long time, and she's learned to

relax here. It's on for too much; they'll never shift it in this market. When she knows there's a viewing, she arrives first thing with flowers for the vases, and makes a breakfast of coffee and warm croissants, which she eats out on the patio. She changes the sheets and listens to the radio, and if it turns cold she lights a fire in the living room. When they come she pretends it's hers — she doesn't say anything, she lets them assume. They compliment her on her house, but she's always careful to let them see the damp and the crack in the outside wall, and they never buy it. After they've gone she goes upstairs and lies down in the master bedroom, and sleeps till it gets dark, then goes back to the bungalow to feed the cat.

One day she's showing this man round — mid-thirties, quiet, won't put in an offer. She's cross because he's taking a long time, and she's got a man coming at three to tune the piano. He barely listened when she was giving him the spiel, and now he's been wandering around up there, alone, for the best part of twenty minutes. She starts up the stairs, the first one giving its characteristic creak.

She finds him in the back bedroom, leaning against the wall, stroking the cupboard door with his hand. There are tears coming down his face. It's quiet in this room, away from the traffic, and cool, and light. They look at each other.

'I'm sorry,' he says. 'I haven't been honest with you. I don't really want to buy the house. Well — I would, but I can't. I used to live here. This is the house I grew up in. I just wanted to have a look. I haven't been here for years.'

She smiles at him and takes his hand. They sit down on the bed and she holds him.

VALID ONLY WITH RESERVATIONS

The woman was wearing a grey suit and black tights. Next to the plug socket was a sign that said, 'Laptops and mobile phones only please.' I pointed at it.

'Don't think I haven't seen,' I said. 'You've got a panini maker down there, haven't you?' The smell of melted cheese filled the whole carriage.

'No,' she said. I stared at her. The rails went by, *tsh-unk, tsh-unk*. I had a good long look down her cleavage. 'Actually, it's a sandwich toaster.' She parted her knees to reveal it sitting under the table, sizzling away.

'You aren't going to stop her, are you?' said a man over the back of the seat behind. 'What harm does it do? They're really good. She's got red onion marmalade and everything.'

I looked back at the woman. 'OK,' I said. 'Make me a ham and cheese and we'll say no more about it.'

Back in the guard's compartment I juggled the hot toastie. The man was right—it was great. Better than a blowjob from a teenage fare-dodger, which is what I told the lads in the pub happens.

As I ate I watched the countryside slip by. I always do. The villages, the farms, an occasional glimpse of someone coming through a door. Fields of livestock, sheep and cows with their young. I like to think of them as for sale, on the menu. I'd like to be able to point to a cow in a field, and say, 'that one', like with a tank of lobsters, and have it served up on a plate.

But you can't.

BEING LIKE

The man having the epileptic fit slid past the window as my train came in. Another man had a hand pushing down on the middle of his chest, and round that calm centre his body shook and swang. It was bit like seeing someone holding a crab under boiling water with a ladle.

I doubled back along the platform towards the exit. I could see a succession of people going up and asking if he was alright, and the calm man nodding. It still felt the right thing to go up and ask, so I went and crouched down and put my briefcase beside the epileptic's head. He'd finished fitting now, and he was sleeping, gasping in great chunks of air and snoring them out, his wet lips quivering like a horse's.

'He alright?' I asked the calm man.

'Yeah, mate, yeah,' he smiled. He was so confident and I remember thinking he must have done that so many times before, with the epileptic being a friend of his. But then before I had a chance to say anything else, he started having one too.

His eyes had gone glassy just after he smiled at me. And then the tremoring: his arms and legs shot out and his whole body started shaking. He fell awkwardly on the platform, and started to shuffle about, like a washing machine on a particularly frenzied spin cycle.

People were noticing. I pushed my fist down on the top of his chest as I'd seen him do to his friend, and tethered him there. It was actually pretty easy. I smiled and nodded at the people who watched. 'It's fine,' I announced, to no one in particular.

His fit was coming to an end, he was joining his friend in deep recovery sleep. I felt suddenly lonely. This must be what it's like for a carer, I thought, all care and no conversation. They looked so peaceful lying there on the platform, snoring through threads of spittle, like beached whales. No one bothered them. So I lay down and had a go myself.

It felt silly at first. But I just had to go for it, and once I'd got into a rhythm the juddering was strangely peaceful. Yoga, or crazy dancing. My bum was wet from the platform. My eyes were shut and I looked forward to the sleep that would come afterwards. I wondered how long they'd leave me. Then I heard some garbled announcement coming over the loudspeakers, a voice but not a voice, the shadow of words, and I thought, Is that what everything sounds like when you're having an epileptic fit?

GOING LIVE

It was Kelly and Abbie that started it. Dressing up on Thursday mornings and jumping on the bus out of town. I watched them from the checkout, and once they saw me watching and waved. A sarcastic wave. So I took one Thursday off and borrowed Mum's Clio and followed them.

They got off at the prison. I can't say I was surprised—well, actually, I was. It turned out they'd started visiting these lifers, who were stuck in there for ages and needed a girl. They were even getting married: Kelly to a bank robber who'd shot a guard, Abbie to a bloke what burned his own factory down with the cleaners in it. A bit creepy, that; but he'd also done a stretch for GBH. It was dead romantic.

How do you top that? I thought, sitting scanning chickens in the cold light of Iceland. It could be in a magazine: *My man's a murderer. I'll wait forever if need be.* And then I had my big idea.

Auntie P had been a medium from way back. I never liked her much as she had bad breath and didn't watch the telly. She was pleased as punch when I turned up and told her what I was after. We talked and talked over a pot of Typhoo, and Auntie P convinced me that Dr Crippen was the man I wanted.

I got to speak to him that same afternoon, with the curtains drawn, and Trisha rumbling through from the house next door. He was a smooth old gentleman—he's American, and everything. We got on awfully well, and though it was a bit embarrassing to have Auntie P there, handling our endearments, I thought it must be like that for Kelly and Abbie too, with the warders.

They come up to me outside the flats, all *Is it true?* and *Fuckin' 'ell!* Dead impressed. Then Kell says her Bob cries because he can never touch her, and we nod and stare out across the playground. Soon we're laughing over steamy letters, swapping tips. Afterwards I go home, and I find I'm not laughing any more.

Long distance relationships never last. It took four hundred and seventy-seven taps to say he wanted me to dress up as his second wife, the one he melted. I wouldn't mind, but—he's never there for me. Legally our marriage was never recognised, but I'm letting it known that we're getting a divorce. I'm back on the market. I'm ready. I've written to *Take a Break*.

POINTS OF CONTACT

Max had always been scared of heights, but when he saw the smile on his son's face he knew he had to conquer his fear. Eddie had been to a party at the climbing wall. He came back saying something about a 'good power-to-weight ratio', which Max gathered meant that Edward was skinny. But the smile was more eloquent.

Monday night was beginners' night. Max turned up in a t-shirt and his jogging bottoms. Trainers weren't allowed, the man said, so Max hired a pair of the little shoes. Like dancing shoes, he thought, while the trainer, Rob, an inevitably lithe blond man with a Manchester accent, was giving the group his opening spiel.

'It's important you remember these two things,' he was saying. 'Think about your hands and feet. Think about where you're putting them. And always, always make sure you have three points of contact with the wall.'

They all had a go, clambering about the foot of the wall that loomed so imposingly above them. 'That's it,' Rob said to Max's ankles as he passed. 'Keep it steady. There's never a rush. You're doing fine.' And Max found himself reaching the yellow marker, the goal that Rob had nominated, and five minutes later found himself steadily placing a foot back down on the floor. This climbing—he could do it. He had thought about his hands and his feet. He had kept three points of contact with the wall. And he had climbed.

He stood cradling adrelalin and pride in the deep, steady breathing of his chest while the others finished. He hadn't been the nimblest — he didn't pretend to that — but he had been in the following pack, showing early competence. Aptitude, even.

They did a few more forays, going a bit further up the wall each time. The third time, Max was a couple of metres up when a woman at the foot of the wall slipped and banged her wrist. It didn't look bad, but Rob took her over to the first aid box in the office, and left the others to it. 'Keep it simple,' he said. 'I'll be back in a minute. Don't overreach yourselves. Just go up to the blue marker like we talked about and come back down.'

Right hand — reaching up. Solid grip. Left foot. Keep it steady. Left hand — no rush — think about it. Find a hold. Push up. Steady now.

Max was so busy thinking about his hands and feet that he didn't notice the blue marker at all. He climbed up steadily, keeping three points of contact with the wall at all times, till Rob came back out of the office and called out to him — 'Oi, where d'y'think you're going,' or something similar. It was difficult to be sure exactly, just as it's difficult to say exactly what the noise is that wakes you from a deep, exhausted sleep.

Max looked up and saw the roof surprisingly close above him, and then down, and saw the floor alarmingly far below. At this point he had four points of contact with the wall, and that didn't seem very many. Three was out of the question.

He stared at the artificial rock an inch from his face, and swallowed back a tear. He was aware of Rob scuttling up the wall towards him. He knew he was going to get a bollocking, and that he was going to have to get coaxed down, in front of everyone, and he didn't know which was more humiliating. His knee had started to shake. And suddenly he felt, in the space behind him which was a hundred and fifty feet of chilly sports hall, that outside of his control his bum had started to have a poo.

FIVE HUNDRED POUND

My growing up began in a pedalo at Carsington Water, when Granddad said to me, 'I've left you some money in me will. Just so you know. I won't be going for a long time yet, but when I do, there's something for you. Five hundred pound.'

We churned round among the swans without speaking. Drifting in near the bank we went under an overhanging tree, and I felt tiny insects or flecks of sap fall on my head and shoulders. I couldn't speak; my head was full of five hundred pound.

Granddad was sitting there, his leg warm next to mine, the smell of his hair and coat. But I was thinking: Playstation. Mountain bike. Year's supply of Haribo.

All through dinner all these ideas were tumbling through my mind. 'You're quiet,' said Granny. It was sort of exciting but sort of painful too—how would I know what to buy? What if I chose the wrong thing?

He hadn't known he was about to die. It was just chance that on the Monday I got back from school, mucky and cross after Games, and Dad was there, home early, in charge, and Mum was crying and hugging me. They sat me down and told me, and the first thing that came into my head was, 'Digital camera. Playstation. Portable DVD.' The second thing was, 'Granddad's dead,' but the damage was done.

On the day I was wearing this dark suit. The collar chafed my neck, and I was glad. I wanted to cry. I looked out of the window of the black car at the rain. My fingers were drumming in my pocket, though. It felt like I had a secret.

At the crematorium I sang along although I didn't know half the words. I tried to listen to what everyone said about Granddad, but all the time I was thinking how sad I had to be, and not thinking about the other thing. Then I found out I was crying, and it was OK.

Everyone went outside and stood about. Boring. Some of the men were smiling, and then some of the women too. They were talking about drinking. I knew there were tables of sandwiches and sausage rolls waiting at Granny and Grandad's, and I really wanted to eat a plateful, but I didn't think it was right. But Dad started rounding everybody up, and I went anyway, sitting in the car next to Mum, her cuddling me too tight.

It was the summer before the money came through. I'd twigged that Mum would make me save it, but she said we could go into Nottingham and spend some of it on something I wanted. We went and stood under the stone lions, and then to Dixons. I got an mp3 player. Then we had burgers at this posh 'joint', as Mum called it. They were massive, these burgers. I didn't like the gherkins. When we were waiting for pudding I got the mp3 player out and had a go on the buttons, tried it out, looked at the instructions. It was OK, but I knew I'd failed.

THROUGH THE BIRCHES

Ray didn't know how long he was out for, but when he came round the trackside was quiet and a blackbird was hopping about on the shingle, not far from his face.

His whole body throbbed with pain, but nothing seemed to be broken so he got up and gingerly dusted himself down. The line ran along the bottom of a shallow valley. There was scrubland on either side. Ray could see the gable of a house further up in the woods beyond.

Patting his jeans pocket he realised he had left his wallet on the train. He could picture it on the table, next the empty cans that the beserk man had scattered when he attacked him. They would call the police, of course, and the police would find the wallet, and this would lead them to Carole. He saw her distraught face, turning from one police officer to another in the lounge.

But Laura was waiting for him in Liverpool, and when the train was delayed she would call, and whoever had picked up his phone from the table would answer. There would be an exchange of information. And sooner or later the police or, worse, his wives, would realise that there were not two missing persons, but one.

This unsettled him. Up till now he had intended to wait by the track to be found, but now, without another thought, he headed up through the stunted birches towards the old house on the hillside.

He must have passed out; when he woke up he was lying in a double bed in a spacious garret. The bedclothes smelt clean, and the room was lit by bright sunshine pouring through the window. He wondered if this was the gable he had seen from the trackside.

She was old, perhaps a little younger than his mother. Her grey-blonde hair was tied neatly back. The first time, she came in with a tray of soup. She sat and watched him in silence as he ate it. When he had finished she leaned over to take the tray, and kissed him with a chaste but unnerving fervour on the lips. And then he fell asleep again.

He dreamed not of Laura or Carole but of the house he lay in. He dreamed the corridor outside the room and the stairs down to the next floor, and all the rooms of that floor and the next. The sunlight and the ticking of clocks in the empty rooms — the house was empty, or almost empty. In fact there was one other person in the house but he could not find her; he walked through all the rooms, looking at the books on the shelves and the pictures on the walls, until he heard her moving in a room he hadn't seen before. And then he'd wake. Often she was there, with a drink or a bowl of soup, and he thought that it must have been the noise of her opening the door which he had heard in the dream and which had woken him.

Gradually he started to get stronger, and on the third morning when she entered the room she found him standing at the window, looking down at the teams in hi-vis gear searching by the side of the track. She said nothing, but Ray was aware of a shiver of irritation in the way she set down the tray of toast on the bedside table. He didn't turn round, but watched the way the search teams turned back foliage and stones with their tools that were a bit like litter-pickers. How they search for the dead. The room was silent but for the sound of the woman breathing behind him. The sun was bright, glaring off the searchers' jackets. It was like the dream. And then she went out, and he heard the click of a key turning in the lock.

CHINTZ ALMOST BEGINS

She bought me a new jumper in the sales. Hang on, I thought, this isn't new-girlfriend activity. But I went with it.

'It's chenille,' she said. 'It feels good, but it'll snag easily.'

'Thanks,' I said. 'I really like it. *Cabbaged* is the longest word that can be played on a musical instrument.' She smiled and snogged me.

I had heard the word *chenille* before, and I'd seen that type of fabric (it's basically wool, yeah?). But I'd never put the two together. Chenille. It was a new horizon.

I lay on the sofa, later, stroking my own speckled-stone chest. On the one hand, it was exhilarating to be initiated into a new world — learning the names of materials, choosing them in shops, confidently dropping *chenille* into the conversation. It was a foray into the exotic. On the other, there was always the danger that it would stop being exotic — once you've explored the undiscovered country, it becomes discovered, doesn't it? I thought of all those names of fabrics which I couldn't identify: *taffeta, bombazine, burlap, nankeen, chintz. Chintz* was my favourite, but not knowing what it was — well, that was part of me. I didn't want to break the spell.

That evening she came round with the ingredients for a Malaysian curry. 'Great,' I said, and wondered if I would be able to pluck up the courage to ask her to do the thing in bed which I'd been thinking about. She snogged me, hard, and clucked over the jumper, tugging it right at the shoulders, teasing the collar.

On the sofa again, drinking wine, in a cuddle: 'Six-letter words in the English language,' I said. 'All the letters occur in alphabetical order. No repeated letters.'

'So?' she said.

'Find them.'

'Why would I want to?'

I lay there quietly, wondering about that. I couldn't think of a single reason, and ninety-nine per cent of me wanted to take her upstairs and—you know—bone her. But a bit of me was insulted. So that was the end of that.

HUSKISSON AND THE SEA

The school bus stops on the shore road and one boy gets off, as he does every day, and walks on to the cottage as the bus continues on to Whitehaven. The tide's out, and the glistening mudflats extend for miles, with the thin line of the river at the centre, and the same pong as ever in the air.

The small, square kitchen has a red-tile floor. There's no light on; the light from the sky streams in at the window; his mother has the same view of the river and the distant sea as the boy has had. He dumps his satchel on a chair and moves round to sit on another one. There's a jug of milk on the table and he pours himself a glass and drinks it in one unhurried movement.

She's been listening to the radio. The light from the sky is enough, but the shadow is deepening. It makes the radio's dial, the pepper pot, the boy's face, vivid, as if they've been photographed by a professional. She's peeling potatoes, and her hands are cold and wet. She revels in it, can't help imagining cutting her finger.

'What did you do today, love?' she asks, softly, after a few moments, for something to say.

'Railways. There was this man, William Huskisson, and he was the first person to be killed by a train. Imagine that, no one had ever been killed by a train, and he got hit. He couldn't get out of the way and it hit him. He was a government minister.'

She's turned round, and she's drying her hands on red-and-white checked teatowel. She gives a little ironic chuckle at the last part.

He frowns. 'Do you think—when he died, do you think he knew what had happened?'

'Oh, I don't know, love.'

'Like — today, when we were reading about it — do you think he could see himself over my shoulder—in the picture?'

Stop, she thinks. Just stop it. And tosses the teatowel over the back of another chair, and smoothes her hair back.

'He shouldn't have stood on the line, and you mustn't either.' Their eyes meet, and his are searching hers for the reason for her reprimand. 'But—nothing's endless that has no beginning.' She turns round again and fills the kettle before he has a chance to ask her what she means.

Later, when the spuds are on, he goes out to look for mermaid's purses and stuff on the thin line of rocks before the mud. She sets three spaces at the table, moves the satchel, hangs the teatowel on a radiator to dry. 'Like my love,' she whispers to herself, then opens the door into the other room, where an old man is sitting, staring into a jolly little fire. He takes her hand and smiles up at her, and they slowly start to get him up to make the journey back into the kitchen.

ONE TAPE DAD

Dad only ever had one tape in his car. It was a compilation of his favourite hits from the sixties and seventies: 'Maggie May', Led Zep's 'All My Love', something by the ELO, a live version of 'Wuthering Heights', 'Hey Jude'. Dad had always been keen on the Beatles anyway, and when Paul McCartney married Heather Mills, that was it, because of our Karen. He sang along to 'Hey Jude' under his breath going round Throckley roundabout, and it was like the world had set the seal of approval on his choice of music.

I knew he'd never buy a new car — one that played CDs, for instance — but I'd beg him to put another tape on. 'What's that?' he'd say. 'Avril Lavigne? No chance. Pretty though. Black Eyed Peas? Had them for dinner.'

Stuck in the same house all year except two weeks in the same mobile home at Brid. Him and Mum going out once a year to the same Italian. Every second Thursday he took the afternoon off and drove Karen to physio and sat in the car eating chicken sandwiches, listening to Robert Plant and the synth solo with the dud note. When I went to college he'd drop me off at the station and that bloody tape would be playing, and when he picked me up three months later it was still on, as if he'd been sat in the car park all that time with the engine running and the stereo on loop. I scowled out of the window and tried not to snap at him.

In my third year I stayed on over Easter to earn a bit of extra cash. Heather Mills split up with Paul McCartney. Nathan banged me so hard I chipped a tooth on the bedhead. It was the summer holidays before I went home, and when I did, Dad was late picking me up. They'd redone the station facade, and I stood with a latte wondering what was different about the shops opposite. Then it struck me: the Italian had turned into a Vietnamese noodle bar. I drank the last of the coffee as it came on to rain.

Dad pulled up in the same old estate, but it had had a wash and polish. I slung my bag in the back and hopped in.

'Hiya kidda,' said Dad, and waited expectantly. I stared at him. I couldn't believe it. He'd grown a moustache.

WHERE IT WAS
COMING FROM

I woke up in the night and was just dropping off again when I heard an electronic bleep—a single, steady tone of about a second's duration. I lay there, waiting, and almost made it back into my dreams before it went off again. I checked the bedside clock. It was 3 am. I got up to look for what it was.

I wandered into the spare room and turned off the printer. I opened the cupboard under the stairs and inspected the fusebox and the timer for the central heating. I rifled through drawers, flicked on lights, prowled the house. I went into the kitchen and stood, looking round at the toaster, the oven, the fridge, the stereo. Wherever I went, every five minutes I heard the bleep, not there but nearby, tantalising, long enough to give me a hint where it was coming from. I stood under each of the smoke alarms in turn, watching the LED's slow pulse, then feeling a gush of rage when the bleep came from somewhere else. I was so tired.

It was an old mobile phone in the bottom of the wardrobe, telling me its power was low. I opened it up and took the battery out, then went back into the kitchen and got myself a bowl of honey hoops. I sat at the table with the light blazing in the night, crunching in its bleepless peace. Then I went round making my apologies—to the toaster, the stereo, the fridge, the oven: *Sorry to have woken you up. Sorry to have doubted you.* Round every room in the house. *This light is very bright. Let me turn it off. Go back to sleep.* Up a stepladder to the smoke alarms. *Sorry. Sorry. Please resume your important work. I don't know what came over me.*

PIECE FOR OBOE

There's just an oboe playing in the hall, with the occasional tap of a woodblock. There's the silence of fifty people, and the warm, rich sound moving over them in a brown wave. On the other side of the building, the car park is full of empty cars. A woman in the third row is wondering if tonight will be the night she cheats on her husband. Things have been arranged so it could happen.

Somebody taps her on the shoulder: there's a phone call. She goes and stands in the tiny office with the roller pulled down over the service window. Her mother has died.

On the way out she looks at a display the children have made of 'The Weather'. Rain clouds, yellow suns, a zappy bolt of lightning. Late daylight fills the parquet floor. In the car park she breathes the cold, fresh air, grateful that there's no one out there. The oboe sounds faintly, calmly continuing. She leans against a Nissan. How strange to have a short burst of happiness, before it hits her, before they run to her and crowd round. The openness of things before they close.

SATNAVS AND THE SHOA

I never thought I would become one of them, the idiots who follow their satnavs into rivers. I don't find it difficult to follow a map, and I have *eyes* to tell me where the road ends. But.

I got a TomTom because I had this new job, visiting the company's offices across the country. I chose the *UK & Ireland* dataset because there's a Dublin office. I sat staring at this tiny screen stuck to the dashboard, despising it. I turned it on.

I stuck to the default voice, Jane, because after all it was better not to get involved, but also because I had had a boyhood crush on a neighbour of my mother's called Jane. I remembered watering her garden one afternoon, lugging a full watering can wherever she told me. I didn't mind Jane directing me to Bideford.

And what I found was that, even before I joined the M5, Jane's voice rather than my own knowledge of the route was controlling the drive. *In 800 yards*, she intoned, *keep right*. So I did. And the signage that flashed by merely confirmed what I already believed. I had The Voice.

The trouble started at Bridgwater, where I left the route for a pub lunch at this little village I know. Jane didn't like it at all, so after a while I turned her off. After the lunch (not as good as I had remembered, plates too big, not enough veg) we set off again and Jane, refreshed after her sleep, took me down a country lane to rejoin the A361 near Tiverton.

The ford didn't bother me, but alarm bells should have rung when we started down the farm track. After a while it was too narrow to turn round and I could feel the exhaust scraping on the grassy ridge between the ruts. But that didn't matter, because Jane was still calmly leading me on.

Later there was a scene, and the police remained dissatisfied for some time with my explanation. It was a very big shed, and why had I driven all the way to the back, and one of the cows was injured, and was there any reason I had left the engine running so long? But none of that really registered at first. I sat withstanding the glassy accusation of a Friesian on the other side of the driver's side window. Jane droned on unheard; I was no longer thinking about gastropubs or Bideford or kissing in the summerhouse. I was thinking about how I would do whatever I was told, and there was no limit to my shame.

THE BOWLING GREEN

As I was walking the dog one day down along the valley bottom, I came across a bowling green. I'd tried a detour off the main path to drop down to the bank of the river, and made my way back past a strange, one-storey building that seemed to have something to do with the water company. There were beer cans in the undergrowth, and the remains of fires. Just as the detour rejoined the main path, the woods thinned out, and there on the left behind a tatty stretch of chain-link was the bowling green. I could not remember having seen it before, although the detour had disorientated me, and the way may have been new to me.

The city is not short of bowling greens. I pass a lot of them, in my travels with the dog. But this one was different, not in the dilapidation of the clubhouse or its desertion on this sodden afternoon, but in the sign that was screwed up on the wicket gate. *Private Bowling Club*, it said; *Members Only*.

That was the stumper. Every other bowling green I know is a municipal affair. It costs a lot to keep a green in order, and the council pays for every one. I once heard a statistic that the amount of money the council spends on seeding and maintaining bowling greens would pay for every one of us to have a heart transplant—or have our bins emptied for a year, or something like that. Whatever it was, the members of the

142

city's bowling greens get a good deal. But that's OK—they're going to die soon. They deserve it.

I hopped over the gate anyway, helped the dog over, and looked around. The clubhouse was as rickety a shack as I have seen, although it had some rather fetching, looping wrought-iron scrollwork fixed up across the front panels. But the green itself was perfect. A few leafs had drifted across from the wood in the storm, but there was no moss jiggering up the nap, and when I walked out on to the crown it was wonderfully smooth, almost flat but for a slight camber towards the edges. I picked up a sycamore key and twiddled it in my fingers. The wind got up, and an old bell hanging on the clubhouse veranda clanged dismally.

Just then I was aware of a presence behind me. I turned, and there was a little old man in overalls watching me angrily from the back of the green.

'Well?' he said.

'Er, hello,' I said, gesturing at the gate to confess that we had jumped it.

'Private.' He stared at my dog, and I hurried off the green towards him.

'I know. I'm sorry. I just—wanted a look. I didn't mean any harm.'

He sighed, and reached out to pet the dog, who up close had softened him. The dog licked his hand. In the other hand he held a pair of secateurs with electrical tape wound round the handles.

'It's not very common, is it?' I said. 'A private bowling green. I mean, do the members pay for the upkeep?'

He looked away towards the wood and hawked up some sputum before softly spitting it into the bushes. 'No. Well. They pay a fee. The bulk of the cost was always borne by the company. It's a works green. Belonged to Wraggs.' He nodded beyond the clubhouse, upriver.

'Oh, that works?' I said. 'Isn't it derelict?' He nodded. 'But you keep the club on.'

A pained look came into his face. He looked away, into the woods again.

'You look after the green,' I persisted.

'Yes,' he said, with a short sigh.

'And play matches?'

He started playing with the secateurs. I had not noticed till now how grimy his face was, but pale too — it seemed almost green in the overcast light of the afternoon. The dog had got bored of seeking his attention and now sat patiently by my side.

'You look after the green but there aren't any matches.' He made no pretence to answer, but stood glumly and impotently before me. 'I bet there aren't any members any more.'

I moved forward in an intimidating manner which surprised myself.

'When was the last match played on this green?'

A look of great pain moved across his face as if he were passing a gall stone.

'August 1983,' he muttered, and I stepped back, my stomach churning with a sudden and inexplicable fear. I turned away from him and looked at the clubhouse. The bell was wobbling in the wind, and the flimsy panels of the walls and the windows rumbled faintly. I saw now that the black loops across the frontage were not ironwork at all but spirals of graffiti; and a jittery rat was making its way along the angle between the veranda and the building.

I heard a noise behind me and turned to see the old man sitting on the ground with his feet in the gravel moat that surrounded the green. He was crying, softly but bitterly.

TENDER IS THE NIGHT

Fifty-seven of us queued all night for the last day of the closing-down sale at Home Sweet Rome. I was eighth. It's a pedestrianised precinct, so once the skateboarders and drunks had cleared off about midnight, it became our private playground. Some guy hooked up some speakers to his ipod, and we played musical statues, then just regular dancing. Whenever we stopped everyone just went back to their places in the queue. There was no trying to push in.

'What are you after?' said the bloke behind me. He was slim and dark, younger than most of us. Interesting.

'Oh, you know,' I said. 'A few big cushions. That TV bracket with the Imperial eagle.' A beat. 'I love ancient Rome.'

'Me too,' he smiled. 'All that decadence.'

So, ten minutes later we were snogging on the other side of the plantings that ran down the middle of the concourse. Of course, they saw us, and cheered: fifty-five of them, accepting us for who we were like benign, alternative extended families.

When we got back in line, the woman in seventh place turned round and said, 'I like that. There were lots of gays in ancient Rome, you know,' and I knew she meant well.

It was a kind of wedding. But, also like a wedding, once your loved ones have got together and approved, it can get awkward. They're watching you, and you kind of feel it will offend them, if . . . Put it this way. After you've snogged a stranger, even if it's nice, you kind of want to go away on your own for a bit. There he was, breathing down my neck. And they all expected us to *talk* to each other, *in front of them*. I just felt this pressure. As if I was going to invite him to leap into my sleeping bag.

It's like being stuck in a lift, I thought, and we're the entertainment. A desert island. Fifty-seven men and women in a boat. I thought of how, when dawn came and they opened the doors for the last time, we'd empty out of our special place and disperse in the shop, and never see each other again. The sadness of an emptied hotel.

THE DIVISION ROOM

Some people go their whole lives without realising they have no soul. Then they get to the division room and a buzzer goes off and they're herded into a separate queue. They have to watch the others shuffling off to paradise. Sometimes a couple are killed in a car crash and one goes in and the other joins the line of the soulless, and they in particular make a lot of fuss.

'But I listened to Dvořák,' they say.

'I read *The Leopard*.'

'I wept over my son's dyslexia.'

'I'm a vicar.'

St Peter shakes his head and shows them the x-ray. They won't believe it. So he borrows a compact from one of the women, blesses it, and holds it up in front of them. And it is one of the small mercies of the Lord that however they stare and search they will never see the terror in their own faces, although they see it in each other's and know that it is real.

WHEN RACHEL LEFT

When Rachel left I started getting these dreams. You'd call them nightmares: I'd wake up sweating in the night, hearing myself speaking the last half of sentences — I daren't repeat them. Vivid, curly dreams, like pub carpets, as if I'd gorged myself on blue cheese and whisky before I went to bed. Which, sometimes, I had.

In the morning I woke up and stared at the ceiling. The whole room was white, as Rachel had wanted it, and the after-images of my dreams would be projected up, like I was a millionaire with a TV screen for a roof showing the works of Hieronymous Bosch animated by Brian Eno. I lay there and watched it till it faded. The fading made me sad, and one day in the moment before I got up to make a cup of coffee I decided to make the vision permanent.

It took a weekend to put up three good coats of white gloss as an undercoat. I wanted the ceiling to sing. Then I went down to the hobby shop and bought a set of camel-hair brushes and a lot of money's worth of paint. Crimson, mainly. And gold.

I did the ceiling in a kind of grid, though lizard's tails and scallops of lace and fronds and beetles leapt over the edges of the squares. In the squares I did stern portraits of the stars — Knight Rider and Princess Di and Brucie and Tim

Berners-Lee — and of course a fair few of my mother and other relatives like that. Sometimes I invented a coat of arms if the person didn't have one and I thought they deserved it. All around the grid I did flowers and horrible creatures, and once I'd done all that I went back and filled in the gaps with writing. I knew what I wanted to say, but the writing took the most time of all because I wanted it to be neat.

Once I'd finished the ceiling I celebrated with a takeaway and a shave. And then I started on the walls — first of the bedroom, then of the landing, and then all over the house. The man at the hobby shop, he's my friend. I painted each door differently: a map, a giant bar of chocolate, the cover of my favourite book, a door. I painted the inside of the bath with sea monsters and the faces of everyone who's ever presented *Countryfile*. I lie in it at night, soaking the paint off my body, naked in the cauldron of the gods.

ALL THE BANANAS
I'VE NEVER EATEN

Perfume in my mouth. Not like earl grey, which I love. Or cardamom. Or Turkish delight. But the sickly sweetness, the tasting-of-smell, of the banana, makes me sick. Along with its mashiness, the texture, the whole unpleasant mouthful of modge.

I'm sitting at my desk looking out over the city's roofscape. There's a big block with railings and service hatches on top, extractor units, and a chimney of some kind billowing out smoke. Funny. I never normally notice that at all. It must be chucking out smoke all day, feeding the clouds that drift over us, doing us harm. And yet—I put up with that, but if you made me eat a banana, I'd throw up.

I used to walk over the Tyne Bridge on my way to work. You stay at the same height, the level of the city, but when you get near the bridge the ground drops away suddenly down to the river. So even before you get to the water, you're high up—looking down on toy cars, on buildings of five or six storeys. Their roofs nudge up towards the bottom of the bridge. You can see the weeds growing up from the joins and corners, the patterns of the ridge tiles. I used to judge the distance, think, If I wasn't scared of heights I could probably make that leap, eight feet out and fifteen down on to a gable or window ledge. And cling on with my fingers. Why would I? Because of the focus. Walking about up there where no one walks, in that small space. You could think about everywhere you could go, at once. And, if you didn't want to share it, you wouldn't have to. You could defend it.

But I wasn't over the houses when the accident happened. I was over the water—not far, in fact, from the Samaritans sign, and that should give you some idea. Over there —no chance. That's what you'd think, and it was what *I* thought, too, when the lorry skewed off the road towards me. I didn't so much jump as fall up on to the rail out of its way and over, finding it wasn't such a simple matter as you might imagine to grip on to a ledge with your fingers as you're flying past it.

And then I was falling.

I knew I was going to die. But it was very cold out there in the air above the river, and maybe that shocked me into thinking. I thought, Well, if I'm going to die, let's do this right, and—I'd already shit and wet myself—I remembered the thing about going limp, and I wondered if it helped to be at an angle so you didn't knacker your spine or send your thigh bones up through your stomach. I went so far into terror that I got calm again, or maybe I just passed out. But I hit the water like a dishrag, and got away with two broken legs, a punctured lung, a dislocated shoulder, a sleep disorder and a couple of badly smashed ankles.

They keep wanting to send me to therapy. To get over my trauma. But it wasn't trauma—if anything, it felt like coming home, like stopping crying for the first time ever. It's true I've changed: I'm calmer, more brutal, maybe. But happy. I can do anything. Some days I walk out on to the bridge and look over. I almost want to do it again. I could. I stand there, feeling my body going cold in the winter night, and force down one banana after another.

ACKNOWLEDGMENTS

Thanks are due to the editors of the following publications, in which some of these stories first appeared: *Flash Fiction Magazine, Fuselit, Horizon Review, Six Words, Stories for Pakistan* and *Under the Radar.*